Chapter 1

The fire ants flew out of the broken window of the humble alley and cruised in the sky. It finally found the Taiji Royal Garden in the southwest corner of the royal residence. It stopped on a beam of a pillar in the Purple Cloud Pavilion and watched everything in the garden, ready to move. After stopping for a while, it saw a crack on the beam, so it squeezed itself in and lay down, feeling comfortable, and dozed off beautifully. At first, it felt that it was lying on the baby's nursery bed, with its grandmother rocking the bed and singing songs to it, followed by its gentle mother feeding it. When he woke up, he was surrounded by many brothers and sisters, and there was a lot of hustle and bustle. He grew up unconsciously and became extremely handsome. He inherited the throne. Then he was sent to lead an expedition by the Great King, his father and siblings, to exterminate the cockroaches who were the rivals of the same generation, and experienced a bloody battle. The memory of the Sino-Oceanic War is so vivid that it is like opening an epic of a war of meritorious officials recorded by the ant historian of the royal palace. It is: the memory is long, but quite intriguing. Virtual is also the reality, yesterday and today annihilation. The yin and yang are separated by paper. Life and death are actually the same. No matter how long you are, you will be silent in the end. The scholar after the girl left. He was hanging in the shadows again. The calligraphy of the scholar's words is so beautiful that the end of his pen twists and turns,

The fire ants on the pillars of the house received the message at the same time. He wrote: "The scroll says that the founding emperor of the Chen dynasty had no children after the second generation of the emperor, so many civil servants and military generals under him raised a kind-hearted and uncontentious royal relative to take over the position of the son of heaven. In the fourth generation, the emperor, Yuan Jia, loved only the beauty, not the kingdom. He ruled the country in a muddled manner and the law was lax. His younger brother, Yuan Rang, was smart and clever, and was a lover. Although he did not have civil and military achievements, he was given the high status of a word of leisure management king, sitting in the Silver Palace. Although the ministers have dissatisfaction, but the emperor's edict, no one dares to say more. The Lord of the Silver Palace, is a nothing, enjoy the riches, but everything can be managed, and the emperor's equal to the king. Yuan Rang loves long-haired beauty, especially like ** full beauty. Therefore, he has long hair prince, lotus peak monk called. A few of his poems can be seen: long hair poem said: beautiful long hair dipped sandalwood bed, soft as water to please the gentleman. Male wind drumming waves a thousand, pushing the boat ten thousand miles navigation. The poem of the Lotus Peak says: "The lotus pond of the fairy is on the lotus peak, the white mist is full of fragrance. The sacred birds do not resist the mountains and hills, they fly around and show their courage. The emperor's harem, the beauty of three thousand, a word of leisure control of the king's harem no less than two thousand nine hundred and ninety-nine. What does this sentence say? It means that the emperor and the king, except for the main wife is the East Palace and the West Palace, the rest of the three palaces and six courtyards of the seventy-two concubines living and working in the ** imperial court, humble servants and maids, etc., are the emperor's women, the alternate maids, are the emperor's playthings. The emperor and the prince can endlessly in the folk looking for beauty, as long as they like, how much there is that how much. The king is not an insatiable person, although he was young and flirtatious, but a seed of love, although not dedicated to love, but pity the flowers and cherish the jade, not for no reason to spoil. On that spring day, he was enjoying flowers in the royal palace Taiji Paradise, but saw that the flower trees, some in full bloom, some budding dew, daintily more lovely. He stood under the flowers, greatly admired, called out: this is a heavenly thing, charming incomparable things, can not make a cold encounter also. So he had a bench set up under the flowers, lying on his back, just watching with fascination. His harem of beautiful women, more than fifteen or sixteen years old, the older ones are also the flower season youth. In his surroundings giggling one stop, the king of idle management only feel the smell of musk, ears warbler, laughter like water over the stream, the body like light moving flower shadow. That a beautiful, feel like the first under the sky to sit and enjoy. What's more, those women, sexually developed, flirtatious wind forced people, in that wearing thin silk underneath, are showing bulging vaguely flesh rhyme to. The king of idle management, touch this, smell that, pull this kiss, pull that hug, think there are a thousand kinds of benefits, ten thousand kinds of tenderness. The moment you can't give up. Fire ants squatting on the beam to follow the scholar's pen end to see here, a crooked eye thought: bulging meat rhyme? Can you compare it with my king? He really wants to jump off the pillar, twist the round buttocks, and compare his butt with the princesses. The scholar continued: In the light of the flowering branches, bees and butterflies around, suddenly blowing a gust of wind, the wind passed, beautiful petals have fallen. They fell on the head of the king. The king only felt that the flowers were like ice, fragrant, and his body was like a flower blanket over his head, which was wonderful. At this time, among the beautiful women, a concubine who had entered the palace earlier and was a little older squatted down and gently touched the thighs of the King of Idleness, and made a musical declaration: "Your Majesty is a thousand years old, you love flowers so much, but you do not cherish them. The king asked: Why did you say that? Consort Beauty said: The flower only blooms, but not the fruit, then it goes into the mud and dust! The king of the leisure management gently caressed the beauty consort said: I am like hands like feet, like skin like muscle, the loss of one is like losing heart. Love to the extreme also. The beauty consort said: concubine like a flower, seemingly beautiful, but will fall, sexless flowers, will wither thinking about lust, is the king of the ignorance. The king of leisure management listened to it, with a hand on the forehead, for a long time, before leisurely said: concubine's words are very true, a thousand flowers, through the heart of the flower only a lone insect, a thousand trees cicadas, listen to its pleasant sound, only a lone person. After the night, the king of leisure management special orders eunuchs, specially summoned to the tent to think about the beautiful concubine, good words to soothe, such as mandarin ducks in the water to make it happy. And ordered the eunuchs to light up a big red candle, shining like daylight, and specially called the painter, ordered to copy it in time. This night, the concubine's eyes with love, face beautiful sunset, body like a wispy cloud, wind up moving clouds, such as hugging and embracing, and the king **, just like the flower in full bloom, with fragrance and exhale, when the petals closed, the caterpillar in the cavity. So the artist was able to produce eighteen paintings, named Gong Niang 18 touches, which were passed around the palace. Idle management of the king's three thousand concubines, day and day, night and well, although more love and more righteousness, but sometimes feel that the heart has more than enough power. But the concubine this night like a long drought to get manna, will not relax a point, and tightly sucking paste. The end like the dawn mist old pine, the evening mist cloud tree. There is a poem "incense burner peak" is good: the twilight pale look, chaotic clouds fly from the calm. Born immortal cave, straight to the dangerous peak. At first, the king of the idle pipe like intoxication, followed by the body around the horse running, and later hands shaking, mouth shouting Qing quickly spare life. The beauty concubine snickered and had a plan: Your Majesty, I am three thousand years fox spirit, one person that is worth three thousand beauties in the palace, if not you have for me alone, today ** will spray more than, sperm died. The King of the Leisure Management heard a big surprise: I treat all the lovers, every ode ** words, are physically act, you have a decadent sound, I have attached myself to listen, as long as the ability, that is, take you to the clouds and fog. How to clamp down today? The beauty consort laughed: the king is wrong! The common saying is that food and sex. Food needs three meals to wrap the belly, sex also needs to be a day to day and felling, can not stop. Then the two legs a tight, a suction force straight through the idle pipe king belly. Idle pipe king shouted, my life is over! Only to see ** blood dripping, wet and stained with brocade. The beautiful concubine laughed and said: how? The king of the idle pipe can only say: fast as this, before the unprecedented also. The king of the idle pipe felt the semen blood underneath, the idle pipe thought for a moment, three thousand years of foxes, how can I afford, if this every day, life will not help, ooh mourning, how to say long happy? Why not put back to the people. So he said: flying flowers are really colorful. You don't need to worry, it's because I usually only care about their own pleasure, not compassionate to all the ministers. As long as you want, I from today, let you go to the people to find their own pleasure? The company's main business is to provide a wide range of products and services to the public. The company's main business is to provide a wide range of products and services to the public. The company's main business is to provide a wide range of products and services. Then they slept together. The next day, the red sun several poles, the sundial turns, the two of them get up. The two of them got up. Concubine Mei was about to leave to collect her luggage. The king of the idle pipe was drowsy and said: Where is Princess Mei going? Princess Mei said: the remnants of flowers fall into the mud and go. The king of the idle pipe remembered for a moment, but he was so frustrated and sullen that he finally regretted and said, "Concubine Beauty, stop. I promise you, as long as you do not leave, I will let you accompany me every day, every day to fight with you, and with you alone, once and for all, the fierce happiness. The beauty consort said: this is very good, are you not afraid of the fox spirit. The king of the idle pipe drowsy said: your suction power through the abdomen, not ordinary concubines, I am very happy, although with blood pulp out, I rest life also do not care, is the ultimate joy. The concubine said: Even so, I do not want to occupy the king, the king can have fun with all the concubines during the day, but at dusk, let the concubine accompany some of them, in order to discuss the joy of the witch mountain. The king said: Yes! He recited a poem, "Beauty's Beauty", saying: "The flowers are as beautiful as the beauty to be appreciated, late to return to the lonely good melancholy. I'm not sure where the water is going, but I'll never forget the sound of the murmur. The beauty of the beauty, please stay by the couch. This beautiful concubine, so lustful, who is she? The company's main business is to provide a wide range of products and services to the public. When I was a child, the young prince was too young to be a man, and when I grew up, there were many concubines around, so although I was around the prince every day, it was difficult to **. Whenever the night is late, the moon is overhead, sitting alone under the window of the bedroom, heart like a horse, body like an ant bite, all feel a fire in the burning. A day or two for years and years, forcing hard to hold down, so hard. The fire ants were sitting on the beam with their cheeks resting on their limbs and thought: "This is really true, it is as wonderful as in the ant palace. One day, the king asked all the concubines to enjoy the flowers in the Taiji Garden, and when she hurried to the flower bed in the rockery, she didn't want to trip and fall and hit a bump between her belly and belly. The red mist flashed in front of her eyes, and her whole body shook, as if she had been a goddess for a while and had gone to Wushan. The experience was as if someone had gently lifted her up and put her down again. In the lightning flash, it felt like she was riding the clouds. The experience was like a kind of immortal like floating taste, engraved in the bones. After that, she pursued the taste of being bumped by the bump from time to time. But tripped once, which there is a second time. The first time I thought about it, I couldn't ask for it, but I wanted to hit something. That day, when no one was in the flower bed, I went to the place where I had tripped and looked for the bump. When she looked at it, she saw that it was just a triangular-shaped stone. So she dug the triangular stone into her hand in the shade of the rockery, where no one could see it, and gently pushed it into her belly. At first, she did not feel anything, but she wanted to find the last time she lost her soul, so she was patient and hit it one by two. So I took the triangular-shaped baby into my arms. There were many concubines in the palace, many younger than her, and she was embarrassed to mention it to anyone. But whenever she had time, when she was bored, she would find an unoccupied place, take out the triangular-shaped lump, sharpen it on a rough stone, and then bang it in her belly. Most of the concubines were ignorant and unenlightened girls, and most of them could not reach the king's side. The idle king had pity for the flowers and cherished the jade, but he did not know how to give them evenly, and the concubines did not know how to compete for favor. The first time I saw a girl, I was able to get the feeling of being a dragon and a phoenix, and this time it was intentional. The first time I saw it, I was able to see that there was a switch at the belly of the person, and as long as it was turned on, it would be a great desire to die. She also understood that the best way to turn on the switch is to approach the king. If by his body that baby to **, perhaps that taste will be immortal flying up to the sky. Because of these experiences, from the palace resentful woman, turned into a day thinking about sex, also dare to boldly in front of the king to reveal lustful thoughts. The company's main business is to provide a wide range of products and services to the market. The appearance has also become more bright-eyed, white teeth, stunning beauty. On the contrary, the concubines were all depressed, yellow in color, and did not look happy and smiling. That day, a young concubine named Si Ting, who was about 14 or 15 years old, usually treated Buyer Mei Fei as her elder sister and asked her: "I see you are so happy, your voice is like a song, your actions are like a dance, and you are pleasing to the king, can you teach me something? Buy Mei Fei said: easy, open the rusty lock of your little girl. Little concubine said: I do not have a lock, that to rust. Sister explain more clearly! Buy Mei Fei said: Tell you, what to thank me! Little concubine said: the king often take me as a horse ride, sister teach me, I also give you as a horse ride. Buy Mei Fei said: Okay! Come with me. So she took her to the garden rockery **: this place has fairy energy, I just got a little here, you sit down first. After the little concubine sat down, buy Mei Fei smiling handed her a stone and said: hit it! The young concubine said: how to hit this stone, not head bleeding? Buy Mei Fei said: do not hit, rust lock in the belly below, just like this, look, here it is! Said and said: I'm leaving, this lock, you take your time to open it yourself! Deep Palace embroidery latitude, the Palace consort is good is poor, some of the young into the Palace, to hair white eyes hazy also have not been out of the palace door. The old complainer wrote a poem "The Swallow Flies" to explain her suffering: "When I enter the palace, the courtyard is deep, the pines and cypresses are cold and lonely. The swallows come in spring and go in autumn, and a rusty lock holds my body. The eunuchs call and drink, and the maiden curses** in and out. The king is not seen, I want to offer my body without male root. The stone is to prevent the palace maids from being reduced to disgruntled maids.

Chapter 2

The young concubine was taught to slowly hit herself after she bought her beauty and flew away. The body, strangely enough, was able to take pleasure, just like a vast body of water swirling in the wind, and reached the shore of the lake. Later, her face became red and her heart was like a deer in the headlights. The young concubine knew the benefits of hitting the stone, and since then, whenever she was off duty, she secretly enjoyed herself by hitting the stone alone in **. I didn't expect that the stone banging was passed on from one to the other and from one to the other. For this great joy, all from the buy Mei Fei, the young concubine thanksgiving, on the secret to take a name, respectfully referred to as the hit stone master Mrs.. When the festival came, the king gave a banquet to his guests. His brother, the emperor, was present. The king led the concubines and officials in charge to open the gate to receive the holy car. The emperor Yuanjia, with the two maidens of the East and West and some concubines, came in, and the king opened the back garden of Taiji Paradise to receive his brother. The wind and strings and pianos were in full swing, and songs were played and sung. The emperor called the poetry class to recite poems on the moon and wind, who hesitated, when the court punished by wine and food. A scholar wearing a goose crown twirled his beard and recited: the Palace of the Golden Palace, the Palace of Ginza, the sky red haze stained the imperial court. Another scholar then said: the wind Queen, the Moon Queen, the mother of the world with the emperor. Another scholar said: "The east wind wants to rest, the fragrance is indistinct, the purple air still rises early in the evening sun. Cup overflowing jade liquid jade syrup full, appreciate the wind and moon long night wonderful. The emperor also ordered: start the dance. When the sandalwood board, drums and music, that there are several dressed up in a flowery palace girls, came to the front steps of the court. When the sky will be dark, the emperor is in high spirits, around the long-prepared big red lanterns brilliantly lit up. The moon was out of the clouds, the wind moved the shadows, and the incense spread the furnace. The end is a wonderful dance to make clear shadow, the emperor on earth. The consort bought Mei Fei to accompany the side, this morning the king and the emperor brothers drink together, the banquet to drink, naturally not without singing and dancing, she has long practiced in the board room in the neon dance to find the opportunity to offer the emperor. Now the sound of the sandalwood board started, she will toot her delicate mouth, open jade teeth, step on the broken foot, and slowly out. The eyes of the emperor, the flow of light. Shoulders resting on the pink neck, shallow against the spring mountain. The garden hip posture, the shape of the oblique swallow, to the two kings while singing and dancing up. This buy beauty fly, due to the collision stone, and then realize the collision stone true yin absorbing abdominal work, deep lustful desire of the wonderful, this time before the emperor, actually not tied **, only a light gown. Dance a few hours, sweat-soaked forehead, wet and greasy all over the body, so the three points of the shape of all in front of the eyes of the emperor, and with the dance interpretation of the stone banging kung fu, that action gesture, all subtle in lascivious, obscene in containing play, intended to convey ** of the wonderful. To be clear, it is the current those pipe dance, striptease. The emperor, usually in the bedchamber, the body is more weak, although ** but the force can not be obscene. If not for the extremely tawdry **, the end only before declaring war, that is, to give up. The first time I saw the neon dance, I felt the heartstrings vibrate, side of the head to the king of the idle pipe said: this brother's concubine is? The king said: Yes. The emperor said: wonderful as this, can I borrow a use? The king of leisure pipe said: brother why say so, go ahead and declare. This is my brother's honor and favor! After that, buy beauty fly often by the emperor to dance as the name, declared to the palace, for the emperor to dance. Afterwards, he was favored by the emperor. Although the emperor's strength is not good, but this buy beauty fly fox charm power in the collision stone Yin power, and daily diligent training, if the natural suction abdominal power, between the exhalation, hot currents swirling, so that the emperor hair, as much as the pleasure of the cloud and rain. This buy beauty fly is also considered to have exhausted the brain of a consort. The first thing you need to do is to get a good idea of what you want to do. The Emperor and the King of the Leisure Management were both relaxed and did not have much to deal with. The emperor Yuanjia, since he was able to buy the beauty of the fly lustful pleasure, every battle will climb the witch peak, seeking the clouds cover the wonderful, even with the maiden and other concubines, is also trying to do. A few months later, one day, halfway through the prostitution, suddenly felt the body hanging empty, heart like boiling soup, as if the wind fell from a high rock, and finally seriously ill. It is: listen to the call of the longevity does not think of the dynasty, gold and silver mountains dark light shine. The dragon robe and jade crown are thrown aside, and the red face with a tearful look. One day, the emperor knew that he could not afford it, so he summoned his brother Yuan Rang to his couch. He asked his brother to be the regent after he passed the throne. Yuan Rang said: "If the throne is passed to the young prince Nuo Hao, there are many loyal ministers in the hall to support him, so Yuan Rang is not suitable for this important task. The Prince was too young to take care of the girls, and he would miss the flowering period of the concubines. Yuan Rang said: family and state matters, the throne is not my ability, nor is it my wish, but the Crown Prince's destiny. I should do my best to take care of the concubines. Yuan Jia said, "The two palaces are far apart, and it is difficult to reach them, so all the pets will be left behind. Yuan Rang said: if the harem to the royal brother to take care of, will let the flowers have their own. Yuan Jia heard, said in tears: hang my portrait in the family temple in Taiji Park, may day and all the concubines hear and see, get happy forever. After saying that, he took the dragon and went away. The king of leisure management brotherly love, a moment of great confusion, stirred his feet and howled, took the young prince and the ministers to hold a national mourning, and then to the harem to inspect. But I saw all the concubines in plain clothes and onyx faces, looking sad and worried, and all of them kneeling down. The king looked at them with a long sigh, said: all the princesses are up, also Bing the previous emperor entrusted, I should take you to Taiji paradise is up. Taiji paradise is already beautiful, because to place more concubines, more exquisite dress, transplanting many exotic flowers and plants, treasures and wonderful things, in order to the extreme audio-visual entertainment. The emperor's legacy has "gold and jade full of wind and moon infinite good" nine favorite concubines, the king himself has a book, poetry, music, song, play and sing eight love concubines, each charming the city and the country, have the appearance of a sinking fish fallen geese, clouds rise out of the moon attitude. The face has a clear pond and waves of the show, skin has a lamb fat out of the box of condensation. The voice is like a warbler's cry, playing the song of the flowing water in the stream. The rhythm of poetry, song and folklore. A hundred herb gardens out of the fragrant, ten thousand surnames in the world topped. Taiji Paradise Palace Garden was built in accordance with the four stars and the seven dippers and the 28 constellations, with the pavilions and pavilions of the subtlety and the charm of the elegant circle. Now add repair, more shape than in the past. Each place, according to the feelings of inscriptions, beauty and cave palace complement each other. The emperor and the king's harem, the two of them are the same. The emperor, the king's harem, the two superimposed, Taiji Paradise beauty gathered.

Chapter 3

hanging incense sickness idle king childish love, since that day after viewing flowers to enjoy the garden, the mind from time to time, the flowers fly flowers fall, it is a pity that ** the four seasons open. I saw those flowers floating into the lake, shallow sink into the bottom of the lake, the heart has regret. He thought, the brother has love, the harem entrusted me to take care of, the second palace beauty people, although a hundred flowers bloom, fragrance all over the world. But heaven has the virtue of good life, the emperor has the love of the people. Let the fallen flowers have a place to grow and bear fruit, to reproduce the people, and to be virtuous to the living. Happy for the world, worried about the world's worries! So entrusted the king's housekeeper, one day summoned many concubines to ** Dark Hall, one by one, touching their wrists and said: flowers beautiful, flowers fragrant, all by the remnants of the fall, why to acrid, now the king wants to let you free, willing to go back, all take the silver from their own dispersion, or farming or weaving, or market or business, the maids can go together. When the concubines heard this, at first they did not quite understand, they were still depressed, but then they smiled, except for a few of them, most of them came up to the king, hugging the knees of the knees, holding the neck of the neck. They said, "My king is a thousand years old, a thousand years old! I am grateful to the king for his grace to let me out of the palace. After that, all the concubines really received the silver reward and packed their bags to leave day by day. Some of them were brought back by their families, some were brought out by the government, and more of them were laughing and traveling together. The first thing you need to do is to buy a woman who is one of the concubines to leave. The king himself, waiting for people to disperse one by one, often rubbed second-hand, pacing the leisure pavilion, feeling reluctant, and even regret. Life's banquets are not always gathering and never breaking up, are they? But the heart is still thinking: Alas! I have done a good thing after all. The scribe had finished writing the previous chapter, and although the fire ants did not understand it, they followed it up with a sense of taste, saying: Once upon a time the ant nest and ant palace had such a scene. This buy beauty fly a little interesting, keep her for the king to have some more babies also strike. The scribe's penmanship is incessant, and the fire ants are attached. The beauty scattered many, Taiji Paradise suddenly clear a lot. The ones left behind are the beauties of the beauties, the beauties of the beauties, some are selected by the chief steward for the king, some are unwilling to go, some are of higher status after being enlisted with a name. The king's maids, servants, and followers are still many people, and Taiji Paradise is never lonely. One day, he walked through the moon gate of a quiet wall, and in front of the rocky rocky hill, there was a path inside, and the stone at the entrance of the path was inscribed with the words "Cave of the Immortals"! He thought to himself, "One bee picking a thousand trees of honey cannot satisfy the four seasons of flowers. The fire ants followed and said, "That's right, to continue the fire ant era, we must spread the ova inside the hips endlessly. The first thing you need to do is to get a good idea of what you want to do. The king is lazy, do not ask the world, thinking, I have always loved idle, is the king of idle management, why to declare me to discuss the dynasty. So casually said: the king of the idle pipe lazy with the dynasty, please the young emperor and all the ministers self-determination. I thought and walked through the cave path to go. Inside the path is slippery, and narrow space, the intention of a distraction, accidentally slipped under the foot, head backwards to go on the lake rocks, the back of the head seems to give a smack. This wigwam, it is to buy Mei Fei in the cave outside the flower garden fell, picked up a triangle hit the stone place. I didn't want the king to hit the stone once here too. Prince Yuan Rang only felt that the sky was spinning, his soul was upside down, and his mind was blank. It took him a while to come back to his senses, and he heard the continuous sound of rolling stones, like flowing water, like plucking a piano. The little eunuch who came to deliver the decree followed, and was also frightened and at a loss. The king laughed and said: "This is the path of the immortals, I am incompetent! The young eunuch picked up the king and saw that the king was fine, and then said a few words to the servant should die and left quickly. Back to the Taiji Garden Purple Cloud Pavilion where the king rested. The king bathed and dressed, and his maid, Zi Su Zi Qin, asked why there was a big bump on his head. The king said unconcerned: it was hit in the cave of the immortals. The first thing you need to do is to take off your clothes and socks and sit on the bed with the king and talk to him! I'm not sure why I'm so anxious to swell? The two women were surprised for a moment, raised their eyes to see the king's belly and abdomen is different, ** actually like rafters firm out. "Master urgent swelling what ac?" "under the power upside down to crack carry on, there is a whirlwind flow inside, tormenting skin burning muscle, non-spray can not stop fainting!" The two women saw the master ** small clothes within the fruit is good fierce, a light touch, hot like hot coals. At once bashful red face said: "Master is to call which maiden into the?" "Not also! The distant water is not close to the fire! You two quickly help me to stop the burning pain." The human brain injury, not timely treatment, the original easy to induce the head and neck straight mouth vomiting white bubble sheep epilepsy, commonly known as sheep's wind. The king's head hit, when the first did not feel any difference, but now the onset of sheep epilepsy out. Only its madness is not on the top but in the bottom, only ** kind of root straight upside down hard, support the crotch tight, extremely embarrassing uncomfortable embarrassment, if you can gently help wipe smooth Xu can be better then a. The actual fact is that this is a special kind of sheep's wind, ** will be confused upside down cramps. Similar to the upside-down disease, or hanging incense disease. It is understandable. The other thing is to hang the incense what do you mean? It is to be accompanied by more than one woman, as if the incense bag hanging on the waist, never leave, in case the attack at any time to catch the duck on the shelf. It is the original and the most effective treatment method. The purple Su Ziqin listened to the words of the king and laughed: master can not make a mistake, the servant girl is a slave, only to serve the king dressed shoes. The tea and water. The king rolled on the bed, face up spasms, only a moment, the crotch smoke, there are things like red charcoal through the crotch and out. Zi Su Zi Qin alarmed, attached to check, in the blooming line through the hole to feel, see the kind of thing strong trembling, sound hair string song, remove the broken pants, white smoke through the place and smell the strange fragrance nasal, let people dizzy. That is the horror of the Moe girl. The seeds are just upside down and trembling, the bigger the upside down, the whole body is bright red, has won the fire charcoal. The two people were shocked, no wonder the smoke through the crotch. The king said urgently: save my life, only you two, and so called to the concubine, my life rest. The two of you have never experienced this before, and are at a loss as to what to do. The king pointed his finger at the two of them and shouted: all the clothes, take turns to pounce. To the divine dew to extinguish the orphan seed root wildfire. Zi Su Zi Qin brain dumb turn can not ask: we two, just maids, where to God dew. At this time, Zisu looked at the king that thing, there is a sense of heart flooded with strange, the corners of the mouth does not own saliva. Ziqin ** anxious erection, only to feel the five inner tumultuous. I saw the king as frightened as crazy. If you do not do it in time, I am afraid to miss the big event, hurt the life of the king, but also in the unforgivable sin. In order to show the love of the king and loyalty to the king's heart, a moment to care so much, Zisu even spit a few mouthfuls of saliva in the palm of his hand, towards the king that thing to wipe. The first thing you need to do is to get your hands on the right thing. The result was a tinkling of spring water inside, which can dip things and help to remove the fire. And suddenly feel the king that thing a hot, the inner wall as if iron store red brazier straight into the pool, is actually a creaking sound, feel the boiling water splash out, the wall seems to be a lot of wet heat rash to, itchy to make people sweat. The first thing you need to do is to get a good idea of what you are getting into. This kind of love affair, is a virgin scholar feel write more of themselves also seems to have the devil on the body. So stop writing. But the fire ants do not care, these are the king and queen of ants ordinary things, what is not enough! The fire ants were staring at the scholar's brain membrane and forcing his mind to tumble and swirl. The scholar also finally to the demon to go too.

Chapter 4

Taichou Spiritual Realm. A huge whirlwind of the Southern Ocean hurricane, toward the direction of the Central Ocean continent **. There is a gray misty black whirling sphere on the surface of the ocean rolled forward rapidly. The weather is very bad, hurricane storm with lightning, the surface of the ocean set off a monstrous wave. This sphere with the intensity of the hurricane is constantly changing shape. Sphere, goose, triangle, boat, plane, cone, etc.. What does not change is its speed, almost uniform speed. In order to maintain speed, sometimes even jumping and flying for a short time. This is the Fire Ant's expeditionary corps, Conqueror I, the vanguard of this wave of the Ant's expedition. In the wind and waves, a fire ant helmsman was holding the rudder by the rudder position of the boat, and four other fire ants were holding their four legs together. The wind and waves were too strong, in order to stabilize the body, the four legs had to add four stakes. The marching director, the big-headed General of Yellow Fire, was standing on the deck armor with a chain holding his body behind him. The waves were beating against the splashing ants, but the ants floating in the waves kept their formation and did not show any signs of loosening. General Yellow Fire ordered the mast to be raised and the sail to be set.

In such a big storm, was General Huang's head knocked out by the huge waves? After the order was given, a huge chimney-like stem was stretched out in the center of the ant boat, which slowly opened up and turned out to be a bundle of rattan nets with a dense and impermeable array of fire ant links. The strong wind blew relentlessly, the waves struck hard, this ant chain weave the sail always stand. The wind and waves were so strong that occasionally the linked fire ants fell into the water, but the gaps and holes were immediately filled by the rapidly closing ant formation. Amazing tenacity, amazing solidarity, amazing fearlessness. With this sail stretched up, the ant boat moved forward twice as fast. After the huge wind abated a little, but the storm intensified and the waves grew bigger and bigger. The ant formation was ordered to morph again and roll in a spherical fashion. As time went on, the ants were collapsing from time to time. Many of the forcefully linked formations, fire ants were peeled off like onion skins, piece by piece. The breakage of the huge ant chains, which constituted the disintegration of the knots, brought about a crisis of fragmentation of the colony. Although the strong wind and flooding made some of the members fall into the water, some of them were blown away and flew far away, some of them drifted near the sea, and more of them hit the bottom of the sea and disappeared without a trace. But the ant formation hugged tighter, the ball core inside the new members of the external implementation of the complement, to replace and reinforce the fallen part. There was a strong lightning bolt in the sky. Cut through the thick clouds rolling sky, in the moment of a bolt of lightning down the ocean surface, the sphere was hit. A large opening was opened. It looked like the sphere was about to disintegrate, but in the process of rolling forward, it soon gradually recovered. Close to the sphere, we can see that this is a thrilling and tragic process. Ant ball in the light of electricity, thousands of ants will be thrown out of the ants, was burned, the remaining limbs flying into the sky scattered into the ocean floor. Closer, you can still hear them shouting and howling and the last struggle before the end. "Long live the Ant King! Long live the victory! The expedition is a success!" These mournful voices rose and fell, instantly drowned by the storm. During the period of patriarchal dominance, it was Constantine, the fire ant king, who coordinated the command. He sat at the center of a sphere made up of millions of dense worker ants holding hands. Not only did the sphere not disintegrate under the level 12 superstorm, but the waves did not even wet the boots of the king and his guard ants, nor did they affect the female ants surrounding the king who continued to give birth to babies. It was clear that the worker ants had a very clever knotting and shape-shifting system that changed at the whim of the king. The system of legions was tightly knit and solid. When we look at the expeditionary army rolling in on the surface of the sea, we see that the core of the ant formation is the king, surrounded by the slave ants and female ants, and the outer periphery are the soldier ants and combat ants. As the name suggests, the slave ants serve the king, and the female ants are the king's concubines, each of which is sprayed with eggs by the king and has a fertility period of half a year, producing 500,000 babies per day. They were the first to be born to the expeditionary army. The number of concubines surrounding the king was far more than three thousand in his harem. The king had no time to fall in love and have sex with them**. He is just busy with the tail buttocks stamp and watering flowers. The king himself feels like he is in the clouds all day long. What is happening in the outside world it does not know. And it does not need to know. Because its master plan policy has long been arranged and designed. Of course, except for special changes. The execution of the king's expedition plan is the gold, silver, copper, iron, four elders and four generals of the wind, flowers, snow and moon in front of the throne. The rest of the generals and paragons are countless, and there are many lieutenants and sergeants below, forming an orderly and disciplined marching and combat system. The large men who guarded the king were responsible for the discipline of the soldier ants, so that the concubines crowding around the king would line up in order to change their ways in order to receive the mating and egg spray. During the march, the transmission of seeds and the birth of new blood is the most crucial thing. related to the existence of the ant corps expeditionary army. The king's mouth rarely speaks, but only eats and drinks constantly, mates and sprays eggs, and enjoys the pleasure of mating and the sweetness of listening to flattering words. Occasionally, he gives one or two commands. The female ants give birth while eating at intervals. The slave ants were busy delivering and caring for the babies, and delivering food to the king and each of the consort ants who were busy giving birth. All of them worked hard and were busy day and night. The worker ants kept on salvaging and searching for food, forming and changing their formations to suit the needs of the king, working without complaint, forgetting their work and giving selflessly. This is a strong and resilient ants' castle, a strong collective with a strong will to fight. They are twice as big as the fighting ants and have wings on their backs. They are responsible for commanding the fighting ants in external battles and killing the few internal violators. In critical situations, they also carry out suicide attacks against outsiders to defend the king. The specialty of the battle ants is to form up their troops to attack the city according to orders. The most commonly used formations are the long serpentine formation, square formation, round formation, prismatic formation, corner formation, goose formation, and flying formation. Self-sacrifice is the highest level. What is the shape and equipment of fighting ants and soldier ants? First of all, the size. It is six feet long, with a broad arm of three pavilions and a tiger's back. The two eyes are like torches, and the two knobby horn beards are capable of scanning and transmitting information from near and far. The jaws and teeth are like knives, and the mouthpiece is broad and convex. The two forelimbs and four hindlimbs are fast moving. Body hair is more than one foot long. Large conical hips can support the body upright jumping climbing and flying. The tail vertebrae not only have poisonous spines, but also can send deadly fart gas. The front and hind legs each have hundreds of pounds of strength for kicking and climbing. In addition to the capacity of the head, the individual form and function compared to modern humans, more than ever. The internal sinewy tubular structure is hollow and juicy, and tastes very much like a lobster from the sea, and is often used as a snack by the ant king. They are equipped with a helmet and a ventral shield, and carry an ant pheromone capsule. The limbs and arms and palm discs are covered with sharp tie hooks. Commonly used weapons are pirate style scimitar, slingshot, ventral poison juice, poison stinger, poison fart and suicide with hook poison needle. Battle characteristics are rounded up and beaten to death. Single combat power level 2, group combat power level 1, overall combat power special level. Marching Director Beneficial General Yellow Fire issued an order: "Riding the wind has been marching for a long time, identify the location of this legion." "East of Lizard Island, west of Turtle Island." "Legion attrition and food reserves?" "Attrition and birth rate are comparable, food reserves are superior." "Change formation and advance to Lizard Island for a full rest." "Yes! Change formation and advance to Lizard Island for recuperation." Lizard Island's deputy general, the lizard leader Lan Bei, was standing on the cliff with a long axe in his hand, and saw a huge black spot in the sky coming towards the island. He looked at the sky, the weather was clear. Looking at the surface of the ocean, it was like before, with blue waves. When he saw the black spot, he said, "There is a suspicious black spot approaching the island, report to the island master immediately. Scar answered "yes" and disappeared after several triple jumps. Greenback, the lizard king of the island, was lying in a coral cave, cooling off under the sea breeze, while two maids were feeding him dried sandworms. Greenback chewed the delicious sandworm meat and crossed his legs and said: "The left leg is sore, the right leg is itchy, both give me scratching and whacking. Poof! Poof! Two sounds, a left and a right jumped on the two service girl, kneeled down in the lizard king legs, give it pounding legs. "Report!" A scar wind and fire jumped in. "What's all the fuss about?" "A suspicious drifting spot was found on the east ocean side of this island." Drifting black spots, not a good thing, Lizard Island had suffered several invasion robberies. Greenback argued up. "What's the wind direction?" "Extra positive one hundred and eighty degrees, that is, towards our island." With a poof, Greenback bounced up, grabbed a few more dried sandworms from the maid and stuffed them into his mouth, grunting, "Lead the way, let me go and see. Greenback went out of the cave, and the lizard soldiers and lizard generals who were waiting inside the cave followed in quick succession. In a flash, many lizards crawled out from the shoals and the surface of Lizard Island. Greenback came to the side of Lanback. This cliff was the high point of Lizard Island. The black spot was more obvious than just now. The experienced Greenback judged that this was undoubtedly a passing transoceanic army. The rat-headed, cockroach-headed, and ant-headed people passing through Lizard Island have all brought disasters to them. Among them, the ant-heads are the most horrible. It is a policy of killing, robbing and eating all of them! Greenback started to get goose bumps of fear. "Immediately the whole island mobilize, tighten the defensive measures." On Lizard Island, there are many minions who are subservient to the island master, they are crab heads, clam heads, snake heads, loach heads, ** etc. They usually live under the wings of the lizard king. Now all the people have to mobilize against violence. Greenback asked Lanback to give everyone weapons, each one a long tasseled gun, that are refined with seaweed rubbing the magic weapon. Many landmines were also planted in the main roads of the island. They were made from the fart bubbles of the captive farting insects. In the woods of the low-lying swamps of the island, in a piece of autonomous territory of the fartworm. They were also recruited for the defense. They serve as a group of fighters under the island lord, swooping down to kill offenders when necessary. Lanback: The island master is wise, we are prepared. Greenback: I wish to rely on the blessings of my ancestors to escape from one disaster after another. Warlord Laitou said: To be invincible, the king's fortress must also set up a heavenly net. Greenback said: I almost forgot. Thanks to the warlord reminded. At the entrance of the coral cave of Lizard Island, the location of the king's residence was covered with camouflage, and swarms of lizards cooed and regurgitated sticky saliva and painted on it. This thick layer of mucus is enough to make the enemy sink deep into the mud, unable to move and waiting to be killed. If dried, it is a layer of steel and concrete, invulnerable to swords and guns. If you are prepared, you are ready, but if you are not, you are not. At dawn, a gale blew on Lizard Island, and a legion of ant hordes spread out onto Lizard Island. The shoals hit and the fiercest impact was the first wave. The minions defending the island, led by Vice Admiral Laneback, fought the vanguard of Lord Constantine's vanguard. The lizards were huge and bloated, and although their movements were brave and powerful, they could not withstand the attack of one against a hundred and one against a thousand. One by one, the lizards were bitten over and stabbed by the fire ants. The lizard minions alone were no match for the group attack of the ants. King Constantine, sitting at ease, watched the battle from a high observation deck built by worker ants, satisfied with the progress of the battle. He wanted to let the whole army rest on the island for a few days, so that the 3,000 ants could have more babies. How is this battle being fought? Is the island overlord really this unbeatable? This can only be described in two words, that is, "sad". Vice Admiral Ranbei was surrounded by a group of ant soldiers. Ranbei held a machete in his hand and took the general's head from a million soldiers. A machete was slashed at the ant commander who was in charge of the battle, and the ants plus dozens of fighting ants were immediately cut over as their heads. As soon as Lan Bei pulled out his knife, another line of soldier ants came. There were also bites and pinpricks from the front and back. The fast knives of the soldier ants saw blood, and Lan Bei punched, kicked, and crushed a group of invaders under his body. At the beginning of the battle, Ranbei danced with his sword, and his moves were well thought out. All of them are never merciful and kill with pain. Hundreds of enemies were killed in one move. A move of the autumn wind sweeping leaves, killing hundreds of enemies, flying up a leg, kicking down dozens, back to the foot, another dozens. A twist of the buttocks, pressed to death countless, mouth a, even swallowed with swallowed plus bitten to death are dozens, roll over a roll, and dozens. Lan Bei was so excited to kill that he shouted, "Those who want to die will come up. The swords flew up and down, and they swung from side to side. The more he killed, the more he got tired. In the end, Lan Bei became a **. Lanback huffed and puffed, but the nostrils were stuffed with ants for a while, deeply breathless. Throat foreign body blockage, swallowing difficulties, and **, spittle all gone, can not say anything, can not open the mouth. I want to stretch my legs and arms, but they are pinned to the ground like piles, squinting at the slit in my eyes, hi-yo my mother, countless body strength of the ants have started a tug-of-war, biting and pulling to split its arms and legs. How dare you! Ran back a violent shaking, the whole body has almost no sensation, only a sense of numbness. Lanback not only began to sweat, but also began to bleed. The flesh was plucked out piece by piece, and at first there was a stinging pain, and then the whole thing was paralyzed. 蜥蜴悲壮了，唱起了一支歌，叫拼死进行曲：咕咕咯，咕咕咯，不怕身上肉被割。Left punching, right kicking, death will also pull the back. Goo goo goo goo, not afraid of dry mouth and no water. Jump upward, run downward, I am the man of the island. This battle has been killing the sky and the earth, the sun and the moon no light. All the snakes and insects on the island were eaten, and the whole shitty air force was wiped out. The remnants of the lizards on the island retreated together into the coral cave of Wangfu. The coral cave was surrounded. It was a good thing that the Laitou army master advised to build a protective skynet outside the cave and coated it with a thick layer of slime. The ant legion After attacking one after another piled up layers of corpses outside the cave and blocked the cave entrance. Even so, the legions of ants didn't let go, and they fiercely pulled and ate each of their brothers who fell outside the cave entrance. The lizards in the cave only heard the sound of chewing bones from morning to night, which made their hearts jump and their souls fly apart. They only thought that as long as the ants entered the cave, they would be wiped out and their bones would not exist. This sound lasted for several days and scared the lizards' timid maids to death. The good thing is that the lizards' mucus dried up and solidified under the sea breeze, and the ants ate up all the ant carcasses and could not stir up the concrete-like gel for a while. They headbutt, kick, bite with jaws, slash with knives, is a kind of all-round terrifying attack. The Lan-back, who almost died in the battle, was lucky to get a life because a slippery and soft mountain snake came before it fell dead. The aroma of its flesh, compared to the hard texture of the lizard, turned the soldiers of the ant legion around, allowing Lanback to limp back to the coral cave with his exhausted body. One step later, the Greenback King would have almost sealed the door for the safety of the whole group. Hey, hey, hey! You said earlier that the individual ant legion was already six feet tall and three pavilions wide, but what I want to ask is how big the lizard was at that time. How many fire ants could fall into its nostrils? It was so stuffed that it couldn't breathe. His throat was also blocked and he could not swallow spittle. Translator's Answer: Little brother, storytelling is the most important thing. The length of the ant ruler is certainly not the same as the general measurement, nor is it the same as that of people today.

Chapter 5

After the expeditionary corps had rested for a few days on Lizard Island. His Majesty Constantine ordered a change of formation, from a spherical formation in the case of a storm to a geese formation in the case of a calm. The direction was adjusted according to the temperature of the ocean currents and the warmth of the wind currents. The goose formation is the kind of formation in which the geese are arranged in flight. The Boeing 777 is like a transoceanic bird reflected in the sea. The form of the Boeing is fixed, the marching geese formation of the fire ant is variable and flexible. The aerodynamic obstruction in any direction can be set Adjusted in time to obtain maximum speed. The Flying Fish Gang's reconnaissance staff officer, Blackfin, reported to the gang leader, Flowerfin, that there was a flesh-scented formation on the ocean surface. "What's the basis for that?" Blackfin sang: It is not fragrant there, the fragrance penetrates everywhere to give to raise. It's not seafood, it's a mountain treasure, the only one of its kind. The flower fins asked: How large is it? Blackfin said: A raven. Hanafin: Is it a black-feathered petrel? Blackfin: No, it's a treasure from the direction of Lizard Island. The master of the Fancy Fin Gang was overjoyed: he ordered the empty group to go and enjoy the buffet. It was the Fire Ant's turn to be alarmed. Fire ant goose formation underwater observation post left to the observation point ant letter transmission to the Constantine king. "Not far from the surface and underwater strong formation of flesh bomb incoming." Soldier ant march supervisor Flying Feather Benefactor asks: Meatball, is it a few fish? Information rotary: No, comparable to strong-fire torpedoes. Ballistic power can break shield armor. The message reached the king. King Constantine ordered to change the formation. The goose formation changed into a boat formation and continued to ride the waves. Squeak squeak squeak! Squeak squeak squeak! This was the call of flying fish, hundreds of clusters of which came to beat the war drums to indicate the start of the meal. The ant boats were raided both port and starboard. This time the fire ants had no room to fight back. The entire group became a meal for the flying fish. The king received the information and changed the formation urgently, turning into a sphere again and ordered to accelerate forward in an attempt to get away from the flying fish gang attack. Flying fish eat a lot, open a bloody mouth, an opening and closing to swallow dozens of ant brothers. Between the opening and closing of the flying fish's mouth, a large number of ants were buried in the fish's belly. The Flying Fish ordered the fighting ants to kill the knot and wrap the chain knot. The flying fish did not stop attacking, their sharp mouths were a powerful saw, all the knots were sawed off in pieces and swallowed into the fish's belly. The fire ants didn't even have a chance to call out the King's slogan before their heroic death. The spherical formation continued to roll, but the sphere was getting smaller and smaller, and there was a danger that the whole army would be wiped out in time. King Constantine ordered the feathered soldier ants to fly. The swarm of flying ants crawled to the outer layer of the sphere and they were ready to fly, just waiting for the command from the ant king. The ant king clicked and ate a few ant bones like sugar cane, and then very calmly sent a take-off message. "Chirp," a powerful buzzing sound, and the ant colony took off. In order to save the whole, the legion gave up many of its brave soldiers. The brothers of the colony, who were still struggling in the water and did not have time to join them, had tears in their eyes as they faced the legion that had left them. But they had no regrets and were prepared to suffer the sacrifice in silence. A few resourceful ants directed their brothers who were floating and sinking nearby to link up and save themselves. They used their shells to close the air and floated on the surface of the ocean, each in a piece, and they became the remnants of a buffet meal for the flying fish. They were discarded with disdain. The flying ant mass avoided the chase of the flying fish gang. The ants that did not have the time to connect and were still drifting alone, not swallowed by the flying fish, kept their tenacious will to survive and their unyielding combat power, and had a good chance to make their way alone on some isolated island. They become the Fifth Column of the Fire Ants' Overseas Troops. Don't underestimate these ants who survived the hardships, they have the cohesiveness of the community and the pheromones of the same genetic heritage, and their contribution to the motherland is sometimes quite significant. The flying fish gang is not a light either. They saw the group of ants flying away. Although they had eaten the buffet, their stomachs were far from full, so they followed the shadow of the ant group flying over the water. If the ant colony was flying at the speed of

Boeing Airbus, the speed of the flying fish gang would be equivalent to the speed of a fighter jet. The clouds that passed over the sky blocked the sunlight. The flying fish gangs could not see the shadows of the ant group. The Fire Ant Expeditionary Force finally had a chance to stop on the water. Constantine ordered the whole army to eat and continue flying. The old and sick were ordered to kill themselves as food for the rest of the soldiers. This was a terrible situation. It was so hard to break out with the army and make so many contributions on the expedition, but they had to disappear just like that. The good thing is that these fire ants are all sentient, and they will not complain even though they have tears. The second and third generations of the group are rapidly growing up and taking over the position of the old fire ants. The new fire ants are shiny and shiny, fit and healthy, and full of expectations for the world. With strong genes and genetic codes, they have inherited the glorious traditions of their ancestors. They will continue to work hard for the Fire Ant Era. They absorb the essence of the sun and the moon, and bear the rain of heaven and earth. During their voyages, fire ants live by fishing for fish and shrimp in the sea and shallow plankton. When they pass by a large post, such as a small island or an atoll, they rest and reorganize their troops. They are the masters of the continental plate, passing through the land, all terrestrial life must bow down. If they get angry, they will implement the three-light policy. If there is any disobedience, they will be surrounded by iron walls and fight a big battle. All lands trampled by the fire ants will lose their prosperity and vitality. In spite of this, the fire ants' expedition is full of hardships and uncertainties. Among the legions of Fire Ants sent from their homeland to the Central Ocean, there were many who were completely destroyed. They were the best land creatures, but in the sea and underwater, the Dragon King was their natural enemy. The Mariana Trench was already one of the deepest trenches in the world at that time. Fire ants had to cross these dangers frequently if they didn't want to take the long way around. High winds and waves, black water, swirling currents and unpredictable depths. These places are often where the Dragon King's palace is located, or else it is the place where the governor is stationed and set up his base. The most terrifying are also those cottage bandits infested places, if you do not leave the money to buy the way, then you have to fight with them to the death. There are many daring killers in the bandit-occupied areas, and even the Fire Ants amphibious cavalry special forces can't help them. Those are the places where fire ants are often swallowed or wiped out. This time, Constantine, the king who led the expeditionary force, thought of a strange plan. In order to cross these places, there must be a ship that can't be dragged down and can't be broken. Of course it would be good to have a submarine, but underwater, if the time for the fire ants to shut down is exceeded, the whole army will faint and lose consciousness, which is a very desperate measure. Where is the shipyard that can produce a ship that suits the needs of the fire ants? Yes, there is. There is an outlying island in the middle of the ocean, a place called a mirage. There are patches of coastal forest collapsed in the ocean hurricane. There are many thousands of years old trees drifting on the surface of the ocean. The king ordered the legion to turn into a spinnaker and follow the wind to find it. Finally found a section of huge rotten tree stumps before crossing those trenches. But it looked like a pirate ship with an owner. There was a black mass of the same kind on it. "Report, there is an overseas column of the past expeditionary corps ahead." "Why do you think it's our Fire Ant's descendants?" "After looking through the mirror, the body shape is almost the same, but the skin is a little darker." "Don't you know that a difference of a millimeter is a difference of a thousand miles? That's ridiculous! Continue to observe." In that section of rotten wood, which the ants called the aircraft carrier, the ants attached to it were brown ants. The brown ants have no ambition, except for the independent kingdom, they just hang around in the gutter of the outlying islands. The fire ants sent a message to the other side, but the other side did not respond in any way. "Send a small team to communicate with them first." "Yes, sir!" The lieutenant under General Heiyu led the team and went there. "Hey! Listen up, friends on board, the Fire Ant Expeditionary Force, the master of the Southern Ocean continent, is passing through your land today, and is as friendly as a ceremony." Because they were of the same kind, although they were not of the same ethnicity, we could still talk and discuss. "Friends? Where are you from? From the South Seas? What do you want?" "Please speak to your chiefs!" There was a brown ant head who looked like a chief. "So it's my hometown. When I see my hometown, my eyes are full of tears. How are you? What can I do for you?" "By the order of our legion, King Constantine, we invite the sheikh to visit us." The black-headed chief looked up and saw a big dark red mountain not far away, a sea castle made of links of fire ants, many times more numerous than the brown ants, floating and swaying on the ocean surface. The black-headed chief is still experienced. He had received stragglers from the fire ant expeditionary force that had drifted to the island from another star. Fire ants have the characteristic of flying locusts. "Locusts fly, fly, fly, fly, fly, fly, fly, fly, fly, fly, fly, fly, fly, fly, fly, fly, fly, fly, fly. The islanders are rich, so food and drink are not a problem. At the same time, they are the same kind of locusts, and after all, their distant ancestors are one big family. But the fire ants became the masters of the Southern Ocean, and their ambition expanded to conquer Central China and dominate the world, creating the fire ant era. The Brown tribe is peaceful by nature and has no ambition. They are afraid of losing their independence and becoming subordinate to the Fire Ants. The chief said, "We won't bother you anymore. If you need logistical support, you should go to the island with us. "To the island? How far is it?" "It's not far ahead." The chief pointed out. "Can you take us on board?" "No, we're not a passenger ship, it's against my Brown Ant protocol." The chief was a bit afraid of attracting wolves into his house. The red-headed chief went back to report. King Constantine immediately agreed and followed him to the island. He made a promise to the public. "The king has ordered, can go to the island to eat and drink enough, not to harass the women. You can have a beach party with a black-headed brown head, but not to be a son-in-law. You can buy a boat, but you cannot rob and seize property. "The fire ants were cheering, shaking their heads and hips and waving their six feet to show that they obeyed the order. The expeditionary force had been at sea for too long and really needed to adjust ashore. This outlying island is called Black Lagoon. The rotten wood drifted into the bend of the harbor. The chief of the brown ants led the way ashore. His tribe followed behind. The expeditionary ant group drifted ashore. The army then proceeded to the landing line in multiple columns. Most of the inhabitants of the island came out to welcome the visit of the foreign ant army. This is a pure **land, not poisoned by war, maintaining the natural environment. The islanders are kind and hospitable. Fire ants find it a fertile land, the jungle is full of fruits and the mountains are full of delicious food. The villagers live in a village where multiple races live together in harmony, and the majestic fire ant team is placed in a prescribed place. The kind-hearted brown ant king received the chief's report and decided to do his best to host the fire ant army. On the night of the starry moon, the fire ants and the brown ants held a fire party in the coconut grove of Moon Bay Beach on the island. The orchestra of the ant army, led by an organist named White Teeth, took the stage set up by the brown ants and played songs such as the Feather March, the Swan Lake Dance, and the solo chorus of the Fire Ant My Glory. The ants were spread all over the coconut grove. Piles and piles of fruit pulp, turtle worms, dried flesh, and mushroom pods were constantly being transported. Fire ants and brown ants danced hand in hand as young men and women danced intimately. Fireflies flew over their heads, illuminating the happy faces of the two creatures. After a while, many live animals were added to the coconut grove, including pythons, centipedes, lizards and snakes. The hospitable black ants did their best to bring out all the things they had captured and bred to treat their friends. The food was served to the young and old alike, making their stomachs full and burping. The moon of the bay was shining brightly. The Fire and Brown men and women, who have not known each other for a long time, hide in the shadows of the grass and talk about their love. Prince Constantine and Prince Brown Ant lay on the beach under the sea breeze and gave each other gifts. They gave each other gifts, including their consorts. They also gave each other personal purses. In the coconut grove, there is a sound of a chirping, chirping, chirping, chirping, chirping, chirping, chirping, chirping, chirping. Finally, the king of Constantine and the king of the brown ants signed an alliance agreement. The Brown Ants not only provided the warships and logistical support needed for the expeditionary force, but also provided a regiment of soldiers to help in the campaign. In this atmosphere, the Fire Ant Expeditionary Force did not commit any crime and the King of Constantine left with his men. The brown ants were able to save their homes and live freely. This is the way to make peace with our people. The brown ant king and chief did not understand this, but they did it.

Chapter 6

The majestic battleship set sail, towing a submarine behind it - a dead tree stump with a hole in its hollow half. The battleship was carrying the soldiers of the Fire Ant Expeditionary Force. The submarine was a powerful tool to defeat the Dragon King. The terrain under the sea is comparable to that on land. There are high mountain valleys, cliff walls, dangerous peaks and rocks, and Kongdong caves. There are reverberating winds in the valleys and submerged currents in the trenches. The Dragon King has a palace built in a grotto in the Himalayan valley under the sea. Shrimp soldiers and crab generals guard the entrance of the valley, and several large electric eels shine like electric pole lamps, illuminating the dark valley path from time to time. The long colored sea snake is willing to be the red carpet at the entrance of the dragon palace, lying quietly and motionlessly. The beautiful corals at the entrance of the cave, digging and red, decorated the rich and magnificent entrance of the dragon king. Inside the cave, the delicate, colorful fishes resemble servants and maids carrying plates of desserts**. The walls of the cave are also decorated with large squid, jellyfish and starfish. Like the murals of Notre Dame in Paris, they are even more valuable than the paintings of Van Gogh and Monet. These days, the Dragon King had eaten so much seafood that he lost his appetite and became angry with the royal kitchen that served him day and night, saying, "You fools, you only know how to make sea cucumber and shark fins and abalone and scallop every day. You only know how to make sea cucumbers and shark's fins and abalone and dried scallops every day. The royal chef, who was in charge of the seasoning, said, "A clever woman cannot cook without rice. The king should import some goods. The purchase manager said: the Central Ocean on the surface of the ocean to see a team, but it is able to conquer the habit of war is not good against the fire ants army. Dragon King: Is that the fire ant that broke one of my teeth last time? "Exactly! This time, are we going to let them off the hook or take revenge for the last time." "Revenge? I'm not that stingy, it's just that these mountain treasures taste so delicious that I want to eat them. I've been bored for quite a few days and I want to go out and get some fresh air. "Get up and drive ---- free." The king of the dragon is very sharp, already fled out of the palace. The main reason for this is the fact that the company is not too far away from the deep sea trench like Mariana. The company's main business is to provide a wide range of products and services to the public. The Dragon King was looking around from the top of the pillar. The fire ants, King Constantine and his consorts, were having fun. The guards of the ants were also celebrating the good weather today. The good weather is useless, the Dragon Lord turned his face, the boat will have to break the axe sink. The dragon pillar swirled in the sky, and the wind and clouds suddenly changed. The sea was turbulent and the waves were rolling like mountains. All the fire ants on the warship were dizzy and stumbled. The ant king was knocked off his throne and rolled down. A huge whirlpool appeared on the surface of the water, the black waves reverberated and rushed, the white foam was the ship's funeral flowers. The army chief, General Feather, ordered a huge piece of wood to be pushed down from the ship, and the dragon lord just had to bite down with a click, and his teeth would be broken and choked in his throat, making the sea lord turn over in pain. This is a dangerous move, whether you are a great white shark, a giant whale under the sea, or the Dragon King, will have to eat the end of the story. The dragon king has suffered a loss, can also be fooled again? The dragon king laughed and flicked his tail, and the huge log flew up into the sky, skittering and spinning in the air, falling down and almost hitting the mother ship of the army group. The ship was slowly drawn into the whirlpool, and wow! The moment of martyrdom had come. The whole crew was killed. The general stumbled and crawled to the Ant King's seat to report the danger. The king of the ants kicked him in the face and scolded him, "You are too calm. The submarine with the dangling tail, all into the shelter. "Yes, yes! I forgot to do that." The general was ordered to go. When all the fire ants entered the stump hollow and took shelter, the whirlpool with its furious and deadly gravity sucked the ship and the stump together to the bottom of the sea. The dragon king was so happy that he took the captured ship to the dragon palace square, swept the tail of the dragon on the surface of the ship, and stretched his tongue back**. The mouth was light, no taste at all. The dragon king knew he had been tricked again. The dragon king knew he had been tricked again. He was so angry that he flicked his back claw and kicked out the submarine, the dead wood pile, which was still hanging by the ship. An understanding and large flounder swam over and took it in its mouth. The company's main goal is to hang it at the entrance of the Dragon Palace so that the Dragon King can peck at it when he remembers. This is, after all, something that is rarely found on land under water. The ocean currents in the trench canyon are raging, and this hanging stump is pecked by all kinds of passing fish, and finally comes off the hook. It drifted away with the ocean currents. When a group of lobsters saw it, they played with the stump as a soccer for half a day. When a group of tuna saw it, they threw it around like a rugby ball. It was the nature of the stake to float tenaciously to the surface. Finally, a few dolphins swam to it and tossed it out of the sea as a hydrangea. The rotten pile, which was regarded as a life-saving submarine by the fire ants, was saved from the martyrdom of the fire ant army. The pile rose to the surface, and the fire ants caught their breath and looked through. Ha! They were riding on the big log that had sunk to the bottom of the sea and was abandoned by the Dragon King, floating on the surface of the sea. The fire ants had a ship to sail again. King Constantine gave the order again. The Fire Ant expeditionary army boarded the ships and marched towards the Central Ocean. But the fire ants knew that they were still far from their destination and could not be happy yet. There is no reference in the deep, dark water, and the ocean currents change in temperature to determine their position. For the fire ants, the best weather for marching is the day when the moon is white and the wind is light, and the waves are not alarming. But such weather is also the day when the ocean gangs open the battlefield to slay. In the eastern part of the Central Ocean, west of the Sulwela Islands. A group of Northern Drifting Damselfish and Southern Great White Sharks came across each other unexpectedly. "Make way! Make way!" "Get out of the way! Get out of the way!" The dominance of the blue whales and the killing spirit of the great white sharks enraged the two creatures. The territory of the blue whale is usually in the northern ocean, while the power of the great white shark is in the warm area near the equator. Normally, they each collect protection money in their own area and do not collude with each other. But whenever the spring and summer or warm and cold currents converge will meet unexpectedly. The two big monsters on the sea floor will inevitably have to fight each other. On the surface of the ocean, the fire ant expeditionary army is leisurely and freely marching. But danger is happening right under their noses. The great white shark is comparable to the old Shanghai beach **, and the orchid whale is comparable to the cottage green forest dart gun gang. ** is a big cut and kill, the javelin gang has a set of 18 martial arts. Usually there is no hatred, purely on the narrow road, you do not like me, I do not like you. The drama of street punks in the ocean. All of a sudden this piece of the ocean surface storm clouds, the fight of the ocean hegemon, suffering the land lords passing through here. Wind and sunny moon white wind clear sea, waves 10 feet high, waves roll several feet. There is a kind of mountain whistling sea of shocking sound, row of mountains rolled over the ocean surface. Lan whale anger through the whole body of the power scolded: good you wild boy, how do not recognize your master it? Great White Shark's response is: less nonsense, do not let the road is to put all of you wasted. General Filippo viciously jumped over the side to the great white shark leader said: have the guts to come over, we two single. The great white shark leader Lang Li Kai excitedly put two fins a row and scampered over. The whale, with its size and strength, thought that the great white shark would not dare to come over, but the great white shark did not declare a war and hit it hard, and knocked it down first. The great white shark opened its bloody mouth and bit down on the left front fin of the whale, immediately staining the sea with blood. General Lan was completely enraged, and threw up his tail to shoot the moon with a bending bow, "crackling" a catapult, a loud sound, threw the great white shark on the ground a heel, mouth yelled: this is the taste of sneak attack. The shark's vertebrae were broken with this blow. So it turned over on its stomach. Phillip cursed, "You're a pussy. Langley Kai grunted, "Don't go away if you have the guts. Then boo boo boo boo sent a few whistles. Many great white sharks on the left grabbed bodies and came over to exterminate the great orchid whales. The legions of fire ants are floating through the scene of great white shark and orchid whale vicious fight. The moon was born at the bottom of the sea, and once it was open and shining. The fire ants were enjoying the poetic mood of the hazy ocean surface full of expectation and wonderfulness. The humble life and the ideal of the magnificent is touching the immortal spark. The chief of the marching army yellow fire said: the little ones, who would like to waltz can now start. Prince Constantine felt like lying in a cradle, recalling the sweet childhood happy time. "Shake, shake, shake to Granny Bridge, Granny Road I good baby." Suddenly without warning of the calamity, like a cradle-like rocking is because of the underwater moment of agitation. Phillip, the General of the Lang Whale, who was killed by many great white sharks underwater, was bitten by the great white sharks to the point of pain, and finally ran out of the sea and hit the ant colony by chance, the castle was shaken, and the wall was washed out a big gap. King Constantine was thinking of his childhood and spraying flower dew on his three thousand concubines, when he was shocked by the sudden bump and shock, his hips contracted and he immediately went crazy. The guards and slaves around him were so frightened that they called out "Good luck, Your Majesty! Your Majesty is lucky! Many of the legionnaires who were ready to waltz were lifted into the sea, and the original compact and dense ant chains were broken. But the disaster did not end there, followed by a great white shark opened its sharp teeth and mouth, biting several times, the ants brothers and sisters into broken arms and legs, many of which were buried in the belly of the fish. At the command of Yellow Fire, the colony flew in an emergency to get out of danger. Ducks! Ducks! The ant colony went away from the ocean, leaving behind a large group of unidentified dead brothers. The whale and shark battle under the water was in full swing, and the ocean was blackened with blood. The moon because it could not bear to see hid in the clouds. In the ant colony's expeditionary army, King Constantine finally came to his senses and drowsily said to the princesses crying around him: What are you crying for? At that moment, the copper-headed elder, one of the four elders, approached and whispered to the king: "I have reported that I have caught a shark boy, please decide whether to eat it immediately or kill it after interrogation. The king of Constantine just regained his wits and said with a crooked mouth: What kind of underwater monster is it? Small shark wagging its tail was brought in to the throne heel. "Which way are you a bandit underwater?" "I am not a bandit is a warrior!" "Whose territory are you robbing today? You have disturbed the sky and blocked the path of my great master's march." "Today it was the great warrior who met the landlord, that's why there was a fight." "Who is the tycoon you speak of?" "It's Lan Whale, I heard my grandmother say that it belongs to the northern landlord." "What else do you have to say after being a prisoner today." "If you want to kill me, I'll kill you. I'll die a hero." "You are young, but you have a big mouth. You have the courage of a warrior! The king will forgive you today." "The warrior has been instructed since childhood that a man should be happy in life and not afraid in death. If you pardon me from death, I will repay you with a ring!" Prince Constantine said: Let him go. One of the guards took the little shark out and kicked it in the ass, saying: "You're lucky, little thing, go! Little shark head a little, wagging his tail and went.

Chapter 7

After leaving the whale shark battle, the Fire Ant Expeditionary Corps rode the wind and waves and saw a mountain peak from afar. But it was verdant and blue, with auspicious clouds and the faint sound of chimes. "What place have we reached?" "It is said that it is the place where ** Guanyin Bodhisattva lives." "Guanyin Bodhisattva is a great god, passing by without paying homage to the next son is a great disrespect." "The king has orders, turn right 90 degrees and head for the Great God

Mountain." "Yes, sir! Turn 90 degrees to the right and head for the Great Spirit Mountain." A thousand-year-old tortoise swam closer. "Which way is the incense, report your name, so that the old man can guide your way." "The Great Ocean Southern Earth Fire Ant Dynasty Golden Palace Grand Master and Grand Marshal of the Central Ocean Expeditionary Army, Prince Constantine, is making a pilgrimage." The divine mountain was getting closer and closer, and the image became clearer and clearer. But see: auspicious clouds wrapped in divine light, smoke and fog enveloped the mountains and boundaries. Under the lotus peak a hundred birds are singing, and the grass is growing by the Yaochi seat. The purple air always comes from the east, the rising sun shines at the door of the mountain, the dense mist flies the crane, the old pine lays down and hangs the spring vine. If you want to worship and make a pilgrimage, this is ** Guan Shi Yin. The old turtle navigator said: "The army is not allowed to come near the mountain, please see the king and the queen. Prince Constantine was helped off his throne, followed by three and a half thousand concubines. The old navigator was trying to pack them ashore, once he saw that there were so many beautiful girls, he hurriedly said: Please stop for a moment, the king, Guanyin Daishonin mountain gate can not enter the large group of people, please follow the hundred people under. Prince Kang smacked his lips, did not dare to disobey the decree, and picked some breast and hip round, climbed on the back shell of the turtle, by it to the shore cliff floating. The Goddess of Mercy is high up in the sky, from the bottom to the mountain, to climb another 1,800 steps. Prince Kang is pious, but no complaints. The consorts could not stand it. While the tortoise was carrying them to the shore, these beautiful girls gave birth to hundreds of ants under the cliff. They also clamored for service and breastfeeding, and the whole thing was a mess. The turtle master who navigates them has never encountered such new problems. The divine general guarding the mountain gate came over and said: Amitabha Buddha! This monk has brought his wife to the mountain, giving birth to many babies at once, which is against the sacredness of the mountain and polluting our environment. The King of Hong's heart can do nothing about it, so he said: "Daishonin have mercy, these living creatures, are my fire ants future warriors. I these Consort beauty ---- poof! Poof! Pfft! The king's words have not finished, those wives and concubines, ** junior, that garden buttocks inside and squeeze out a lot of ants baby. Lotus seat on the bodhisattva wise eyes divine light scanned to these sights, so up the seat to the mountain. The Buddha's wise eyes scanned these scenes, so he got up and came to the bottom of the mountain. He came out of the mountain gate and said to Prince Constantine with a benevolent face at the edge of the cliff: "The throne has sailed far, it has been a lot of hard work. Prince Konstantin fell down and worshiped him, saying, "Please accept a bow. The Grand Master said: "The war in Central China is inevitable, I hope you have compassion, less killing and more releasing. After saying that, a breeze disappeared. Prince Kang and worshiped the air two worship said: the next king to remember. It was hard for the god of the mountain gate to carry all the children born by the ant concubines onto the back shell of the old tortoise, and to carry them to the ant group. The King, with a sweep of his jaws, stuffed them into his own mouth and swallowed them. The turtle master watched, in the heart straight chanting Amitabha Buddha. The tiger's poison does not eat its children. The domineering and murderous aura of the king who leads the expeditionary army is really too heavy. May all beings be fortunate enough to avoid the calamity. *** under the sacred mountain, there is a direct highway *** Dragon King Dragon Palace, this a warm and far away from the current, the daily passage of countless fish soldiers and shrimp, like the modern restaurant Vancouver crabs, lobsters, eels are in the current rush to and fro. Of course, there are also cases of large fish such as blue and green dueling, green and white mixed battle. There are also robbers and bandits in the crooked pass of the highway, the corner of the turnpike, and the small off-ramp, stopping the merchants for money. The expeditionary army of King Constantine's ant regiment ran into such a situation, and the land monster ran into the water monster. On the fifth day after the king's pilgrimage, a group of sea squid ambushed a cave in a mountain pass in the crowded temperate ocean stream. The bandit at the head of the group was one foot tall, with legs stretching two feet and a head circumference of eight feet. The legion was moving forward when this group came out of the water and blocked the way. The outpost observer reported to the army director General Huang Huo: there are three roadblockers blocking the way, past experience from the shape of the pirate squid. The information reached the four elders beside the king. "Brake, stop the advance!" The order came down, and the ant group drifted close to the surface of the water. The four elders of gold, silver, copper and iron and the four generals of wind, flower, snow and moon discuss the situation of the pirate in front of them. "This pirate barely with no armor, send a team of flying ant special forces to exterminate its head." "The long silk leg is a great threat to the legion, or pay some money for the road with peace." "This is not in line with the style of the fire ants who want to make the world subservient." "The first time to cut off his long legs." "The pirate is not a long leg, there are more legs, can not cut off many at once." "Underwater thieves more than some unknown habits, know your enemy!" "Sea squid have like to dance hobby, why not legs and it to a dance music." "What kind of dance music can attract it?" "The beautiful crane dance is unforgettable, and the dance is simply wonderful. The king of Constantine has a talented luthier by his side, because from time to time the king's beautiful ladies have to sing and dance to the king to flatter him, in order to care for the spraying of eggs, in order to be able to give birth to ant babies to secure their position as consort. "Call the luthier." The luthier, with white teeth, came out singing and dancing. "There are challenging war drums beating outside, make a dance to distract some arrogant sea squid who don't know how to discipline themselves." "The post has heard the lord say Swan Lake, this is a ready-made old tune." "Take your band with you and try outside." "Tally! Listen to the group in front, here is the territory of Master Wu, quickly leave the money to buy the way, let you pass, or die a death of there." The squid gang thumped their fat white stomachs and impatiently passed the word. "Yes! Yes! Come on! Don't hurt the peace yet, have fun, have fun." The fire ant's microphone passed the word to soften the blow. The white-toothed luthier unhurriedly directed the orchestra to line up, tune the strings, and blow the trumpet, followed by a burst of winged music, and then the Swan Lake dance. When the music started, the bandits were really dizzy as if they had been drinking wine. "Tally! You guys are really something, what kind of dance music is this? It's mesmerizing." The bandit leader said. "The squid dance song! Sing and dance, you guys!" The white-toothed luthier confused the squid by referring to the swan dance as the squid dance. Several intercepting squid could not help but twist and turn. The music of the squid dance is a bit interesting: bang bang bang, bang bang bang, bang bang bang, bang dong dong dong dong dong dong dong dong dong dong dong. One foot short, one foot long, I am in the middle of the sea, eat small fish, plus small shrimp, grow white and fat. I like the wind, I like the rain, I am a big dancing burgher, you dance, I dance, I dance, hug as a bridesmaid. With the dance music, the fire ant legion drifted with the wind, and soon left, several squid forgot the task given to them by the boss, with large round monk's head, stretching out the worm-like cartilaginous ribbon-shaped long feet, as if not even wearing triangle **, they wiggled their asses and danced in the surface of Zhanlan. The three sea squid, one above the water, one under the water, forgetting to sing and dance vigorously, drifting and jumping, a group of squid minions underwater, happy to form a round formation, also twisting waist, are happy to drift and jump dizzy. When they came to their senses, the robbed masters had long gone away. When this wave of fire ants sent their expeditionary forces to the Central Ocean continent, the Rat Head Axis Alliance and the Cockroach Mutation Alliance also increased their troops to the Central Ocean continent. During the Three Thousand Year War, the territory of the Central Ocean Continent was divided into three pieces. The Fire Ants were stationed in the eastern part of the Central Ocean in the hilly Erjiang region, the Cockroaches were stationed in the Sanchaikou region, the home of fish and rice in the plains, and the Ratheads occupied the vast grassland area in the mountains of the Sea of Clouds. The common feature of the three regions is that they are all good for defense and better for offense. They all wanted to swallow the foreigners in one fell swoop. If any one of the three parties in the battle for the Central Ocean loses, the balance of power will be broken. Will make the other side is also eaten by the other strong, thus creating a situation where one side dominates. At that time, the dominant party will send an army to sweep the continental plates, and will be invincible with the unparalleled advantages of the Central Ocean continent. If the creatures on each plate do not surrender and submit, they will be exterminated and die. The three armies of ant-heads, rat-heads and cockroaches will gather in the Middle Continent. The decisive battle is inevitably coming. The ant-head commander, Marshal Gradin III, has as his chief of staff the second wise master. He has a large number of fierce generals under his command, strict military discipline, bright armor, sufficient provisions, and a complete arsenal. Governor You You, the commander of the cockroach-headed army, hired General White Ruler of the Moth-headed allied army as the first think tank. The members of the think tank include senior and outstanding commanders of allied armies. He is good at training special forces. He was the best at breaking attacks, tunnel warfare, and special warfare at night. The Rat Head Commander, Prince Ao Dai, has an excellent and noble intelligent bloodline, and has four major commanders under him, namely, the Grey, White, Fragrant and Stinky, each leading the Grey Head, White Head, Pintail Head and Skunk Head of the Rat Corps. Atmospheric smoky, proud of the group. The three commanders all know that the duel in the eastern continent of Central Ocean will be a battle to determine the world. Let people fear excited and yearning. Billions of years ago, biological survival competition and intelligent people fighting for world domination of the conquest behavior how similar Naier, but exquisite, dripping, a thousand changes in strategy and tactics demonstrate the adaptation to the non-stop changes, is the objective law of survival competition to win. The war began with a letter of absolute declaration of war from the rat commander's office. This letter of war was written by the rat-headed Ao Xiong, and its main idea was as follows: "For the good man, the clear man does not do the dark thing, for the master of the absolute kill the other side to submit. The opponent gives up resistance to gain a chance to live, and resists in vain to die. Now the warriors have gathered, and a million troops are waiting for orders to be sent. The army is so wise and strategic that there is no one left to take chances. With gratitude, we will receive all the friendly peoples in our march. No matter how many ants or cockroaches surrender, they will surrender as soon as possible. The wise thing to do is to break your heart and collect your bones. If not, life and soul will be in ruins and never recover. "The rat head is obviously a cunning and deceitful person, but he pretends to be a generous and frank teacher, using clever words to confuse the public. After receiving the war letter, the generals and soldiers shouted their displeasure at Rat Head's aggressiveness at the fire ants' base camp. At the same time, they were actively preparing for the battle against the black clouds overwhelming the city. Marshal Gladin: I would like to ask the advice of the Master of the State for his advice on how to deal with the situation. The Chinese government has been working hard to improve the situation. The cockroaches are in the land of fish and rice, and they have the laziness of eating all day long. The gray rats are running around the grasslands and have the disadvantage of loose personalities. However, if any one of the three sides starts an army, the other side will definitely take advantage of the situation. It is necessary to have a clam fighting with each other in order to make a profit. I would like to go to the cockroach camp and persuade them to lead their troops to fight with the rat head, and our army will then cover up and kill them, so that we can get twice the result with half the effort. "The rat and cockroach people have no integrity and are selfish and scatterbrained, so they can hardly do anything righteous." "If you tell them what is good and what is right, how dare you disregard the pain of **?" "How can you return in one piece when you are going to an enemy country and the journey is difficult and the lobbying is not easy?" "The former captured a battalion of the moth-headed beauty of the cockroach governor of You You You, who has always been favored with a big ass, is now returned in the name of escort. The governor of You You is fond of beautiful girls, and the general of Moth Head and White Ruler is the first wise man, so he cherishes her by nature. I can't let it not see the guests. "If we can convince the cockroaches to attack first and make the duel rehearsed, I, the fire ants, will take advantage of the gap to kill the rats and get the name of rescuing the cockroaches and become a benevolent teacher! The two of them laughed out loud and clapped their hands, saying that it was wonderful. The next day, with a beautiful breeze and clear clouds, Master Zhigao took four winged guards and a party of five men to cross from the Second River to the east by reed leaf, and went down the river to the headquarters of the cockroach monster at the mouth of the Third River.

Chapter 8

There is a poem that says: "The mind is not confused after planning, the footsteps of the mangled plain are wide. The mountains and rivers are winding to the top and going, what can be happy with victory and profit! A general can lead a million soldiers, a plan to set the society at ease. A thousand wonders and monsters are subservient, and they cheer from the bottom of their hearts**. This wise master is a piece of earwax hooked out by the little finger of the Star of Creation under the command of the Earth Star Lord. On this day, he entered the cockroach-headed monster's control area. We arrived at the headquarters of the cockroach-headed monster at the cliff. The schoolmaster reported to us that General Ji Gao of the Ant Head Command was visiting us. When Governor You You heard the report, he asked the White Ruler: What is the mystery of the old demon coming here uninvited? The moth monster White Ruler said: I'm afraid it's not simple. You You You said: Motherfucker! Ordered the sword and axe man to remove one of his arms first before making sense. White ruler twirled his whiskers and said: the governor should not be reckless, or there may be important military information is not known, and first ordered him to come in before talking. But I saw a flash of red light, Zhi Gao Guo Shi and his five people came outside the tent. They were surrounded by cockroach soldiers, who seemed to be waiting for their orders, and at the order of the governor, the ants would be cut into pieces. The man was calm and collected, saying: "I am happy to have a guest from afar. You You You barbarously said: not a guest, is a red-headed monster! The white ruler at the edge of the seat said: I wonder what advice to come from afar, is the war letter? Ji Gao laughed and said: "We will send a small school to make a war declaration. I heard that you are not enough soldiers, now the gentleman has the beauty of adults, send back to your army in the tent of the big hip can nurture beautiful girl a camp, would like to accept? The first time you hear, turn anger into joy said: there is this good thing, but to thank the goodwill. White ruler said: two armies at war, not to cut women and children. New atmosphere and new style. I thank you on behalf of You You Yu's grandfathers. The atmosphere became better in the second place, Zhigao Guoshi said: the war letter from the rat-headed monster, the words are wild, the behavior is outrageous, it is necessary to thwart its sharpness to calm the hate. The rat army will not be killed enough to promote the army's prestige. Now the two rivers decided to advance and retreat with the Sanchaikou in order to put an end to the rat infestation in the mountains of Yunhai. I don't know what the governor and the state teacher think? A gray-headed moth in the class of white ruler said, "We have always fought separately from you, but why do you offer your beauty to the door to talk about the project? If we weren't afraid of the rat-headed monster's strength, why would we have come to visit? Another flower-headed advisor said, "In the recent battle, you fire-headed ants killed 30,000 of my soldiers, and now you are sending back a small camp in an attempt to make friendship. Zhigao said: "There are bound to be casualties in a battle. The return of the beauty of the girl, are a hundred miles to pick a big buttocks, the day after the governor of the spray, not only to enjoy the pleasure of bed, but also a short period of time can be 30,000 newborn number, the recent months of continuous rains, the two rivers and three branch river flooding, the cockroach army in the lower reaches of the death of countless people, the return of the beauty of the girl is actually to strengthen your strength, such good intentions do not know ah! Now the rat-heads think they have the geographical advantage of the Yunling Mountains and want to take advantage of the opportunity to kill us. If Sancha River does not join hands with the two rivers, they will be slaughtered, the lips will die, the teeth will be cold, the cockroaches will disappear, and only the rats will be big. There is another gray-headed participant said: "The rat head is arrogant, indeed, based on strength, supported by military equipment, and supported by the vast number of submissive people in the territory, and is determined to raise an army to unify the world, collect taxes and taxes, and conquer the four directions. Now that our region is flooded, our soldiers and people are damaged, and our walls are crumbling, we should try to do it slowly and retreat to advance. You ants-headed monsters, want to take advantage of the danger of people? Another wise man said: "Without strong armor, it is difficult to yield to man's army. Now I am flying, climbing, fleeing, jumping, the four special soldiers, behind the enemy's back in great hardship, in great need of military assistance, now Sancha River is flooded world, military equipment security difficulties, unfavorable and rat monster head-on battle. Zhigao sat on the tai shi chair and laughed and said: this kind of causality is the view of the harp. The rat monster seems to be strong and strong, but it is selfish and self-serving, despise the masses. Why should we be afraid of a scattered mess? Now I have a decisive strategy, the fire ants and you all join hands, not only to save you from danger and hardship, but also to kill the rat-headed monster without returning. You You You twirled your beard and said, "I would like to hear more about it. The cockroach-headed army is famous for its special warfare function, and it is often difficult to defend itself behind enemy lines. If we give up the harassment behind the enemy, the rat-heads will concentrate their forces for a quick victory and come out in empty groups. The mouth of Sancha is right in front of Rat Head's eyes, so instead of being beaten passively, we should take the initiative to attack. The fire ants are willing to attack from a long distance, although they are tired and exhausted, but they can be covered behind, so that they can be frustrated and have the effect of a surprise attack. But if we lose 50,000 troops a day in a head-on battle, we will lose hundreds of thousands of troops in a few days. The company's main goal is to make sure that the company's products and services are available to the public. The military tent was discussing the situation in Central China and the countermeasures. Suddenly, the sound of drums and music came from outside. The schoolmaster came to report that some white moths and beautiful girls had been sent to the port by the Fire Head Army. The governor of You You was delighted to hear that, and then called into the tent, but saw a dozen beautiful women are sent by Zhigao Guo Shi, arrived first. The beauty girls returned to the camp door, a change of sad and sad face, each happy and joyful. When they arrived at the tent of the army, they firstly said "Hurray" to the governor, and then they said that they missed their homeland. The woman's face, charming body, round buttocks swaying, charming posture, the cockroach head in the tent of the army and other male citizens disturbed the heart, can not help themselves, can not help themselves. Ji Gao twirled his whiskers and laughed. Governor Yuyou, the white ruler, made a happy decision when he felt like it: to make a temporary agreement with the fire ants. It was decided that the cockroach-headed army would first attack the rat monster in the vicinity of the city. The ant-headed army would run far away from the enemy's belly. The battlefield is located on the vast alluvial plain at the mouth of the Sancha River. The day of the general attack was set for the night when the moon was full. Within two days, a battalion of E Tau beauties arrived one after another, and the governor was "embarrassed" to have occupied the majority of the middle-army tent, while the rest of the white rulers and think-tanks and generals had more or less. Some received a dozen, some received a few, at least one or two. It was a great joy for all. The cockroach army celebrated the return of Meiji with a feast, and the soldiers and people in Sanchahekou celebrated together with candles, candles and fireworks for several days. After the banquet, Ji Gao and Yu Yu and White Ruler left behind two liaison officers of the feathered ant-heads and returned home with their orders. Zhigao returned to the king of Gladin and told him what had happened. The king was overjoyed and ordered the whole army to prepare for the big battle. Although the cockroach head had promised to attack first, the rat-head army was not easy to deal with, and the fire ants had prepared two more lethal weapons. First, in order to kill the rat and cockroach heads, the fire ants have already cultivated a secret weapon, a ldh flea worm, which is called a poisonous witch in a secret place. By putting a lot of fleas into the rat colony and infecting them with each other, it could almost kill the rats. The second kill was to lure the rats to meet the cockroaches at the mouth of the Sancha River and activate the dam of the two rivers to flood the alluvial plains downstream. In one fell swoop, the two armies of rats and cockroaches were eliminated from the grass and mud. This is a top secret A plan. Since the battle situation is that you have me and I have you, there is an interlocking of teeth. The key to victory for the fire ants is spy prevention. The following game is Fire Ant Battle Mouse Cockroach 007, divided into two parts. One is to smuggle the poisonous witch. The second is to eliminate the rat and cockroach hackers. If these two games are played well, it becomes the destiny of Fire Ant to dominate the world. For the sake of narrative convenience, let's say that Fire Ant has achieved great success with first-class anti-spy measures. This is because the Great War in the Fire Ant Era is the focus of our description. The Cloudy Ridge is a hilly area above sea level. In the middle there is a drought-protected plain. There are two mountain passes in the east and west to ensure the smooth flow of the monsoon. Thanks to this geographical advantage, rat-heads proliferated. Castles were built on the plains and outposts on the hills. The open spaces were filled with fruit trees and crops that had existed since time immemorial, and they continued to grow year after year for generations. The indigenous inhabitants, including the jackals, wolves, tigers and leopards on the mountains, the snakes and insects on the plains, and the falcons and birds of prey in the sky, were all wiped out, except for those who willingly submitted. Finally, the subjugated birds were forced to submit because the ground was occupied by rats, and they were unable to land at night and day. The ferocious tigers and leopards were first killed by night attacks during sleep because of their pride and rage, and the plains could not survive and had to hide in the mountains. After unifying the Yunhai Mountains, the rat-heads moved to the Erjiang area and the Sancha River estuary, but were met with determined resistance from the ant-heads and the cockroaches. Although there were victories and defeats in the war between the Rat Head and the Ant Head, the Ant Head penetrated into the Yunhai Mountains and kept defeating the Rat Head, so that the Rat Head regarded the Ant Head as a big problem in its heart. The cockroach army, which was considered the most insignificant by the Rat Head, was found to be a different species from the ordinary creatures after years of conquest. The original long-term coexistence to become enemies to each for the survival of the vow not two. The long-standing grudge has turned into a struggle between you and me, which has been accumulating for 3,000 years. The only way to enjoy the prosperity and reassurance of world domination is to completely defeat and destroy each other. It is still unknown who will die. It has become the consensus of all three parties to carry out the extermination of the other side and to settle the world in one battle. Each other are looking for the opportunity to duel, each other from the East, South, Western home to increase troops in the ocean. Thousands of years are just a snap of the fingers. Because at that time, millions of years were used as the calculation cycle. A huge lake in the upper reaches of the Erjiang River basin, called Mumba Lake, had enough water to wash away the Erjiang River and flood the Sancha River area downstream. Since occupying the area and discovering the secret, the fire ants have been carrying out a thousand-year project. Relentlessly digging through the rock quarry, determined to attract water. Now that the project is nearing its end, luring the enemy to the Erjiang and Sancha rivers has become a priority, and the thousand-year secret project will be revealed. The smug rat and cockroach heads have no idea that danger is approaching and that a catastrophe is about to happen. To realize this plan, the fire ants have moved all the citizens to the half-slope. On the half-slope, they forge tools for dredging and quarrying, and make vehicles for transport, which, it is important to understand, are not vehicles in the modern sense of the word and forge manufacturing methods. But the purpose was the same. With a battalion of beautiful women and clever arguments, Chico convinced the cockroach governor and his wise men, but not nearly enough in a strategic sense. He was determined to send another mission to Rat's Head to instigate Prince Ao Dai and Master Ao Xiong to send troops to Sancha River. Set the battlefield of the Sino-Oceanic War in the alluvial plain of Sancha River. Is the most important. Master Zhigao had a favorite pupil, Chai B, who was 20 years old and had a face like a crown, and was a good man **, and had a deep understanding of Master Zhigao's strategy of battle. Zhigao decided to send him to the Cloud Sea Cave in the Cloud Sea Mountain Range instead of himself, and the arrogant and arrogant Ao Xiong. As long as Ao Xiong trusts him, there will be no more suspense for Lord Ao Dai.

Chapter 9

The rat's head colonizes the cloud and sea mountain, looking out at all beings in the domain, but its fatal weakness is greediness. When he is tempted with profit, he is tempted by his heart, and his desire is born in his guts. Zhigao decided to give away 20 large carts of jewels at great cost. He also gave away the vehicles, a unique and exclusive invention. At the foot of the mountain, the workshop was scattered and the sound of pounding was incessant. The metallurgical furnaces are kept burning day and night. In the ant tunnels at Mumba Lake, fire ants move in and out in a line. Trucks and trucks of soil and rubble are transported out of the tunnel. Day and night, the dredging project is a source of hope for the future. "Report! There is a messenger from the ant-headed monster asking for an interview." The Cloud Sea Cave is secluded and heavily guarded, so the old ant-headed monster is asking for an audience, which is something new. The rat-headed Ao Dai king master listened to a little joyfully to Ao Xiong state teacher said: there is a surrender form to come. The Aussie Master bared his teeth and smiled, and said, "I'm afraid it may be a tribute for peace. A large, cleverly disguised car lined up in the aisle of the cave and a dusty, beautiful man jumped out of the car, followed by a team of bodyguards. The rat-headed king looked up from his throne and saw the fire-colored ant-headed monster: bright eyes looking like lightning, horns moving like a long sword, wide mouth with steel teeth showing sharp edges, body hair as red as fire. The front limbs and back arms stand like piles, and a sharp buttock is in the middle of clrotum, and the two feathers on the back are not opened and closed, so the domineering spirit is exposed to show its majesty. The rat eunuch at the side of the king was screaming twice in a squeaky voice, meaning that the ambassador was kneeling to see the king. Gui B stepped forward a few steps, pointed buttocks a support, and even turned a few heels, to the rat king's seat bowed and bowed an arch, said: the fire ants marshal tent special envoy Gui B meet the king. "Don't be polite and sit down!" "This envoy is ordered by the commander to make peace with the rat neighbors, and to give a copy of the form, 20 valuable gifts and jewels." Ao Dai rat master has long glanced at the red-haired six-legged monster behind a long slip of things, heard that it is a gift to the cave, the two canine teeth a bared: what gift? You are very polite. Gui B., with a chapter in his hand, recited aloud to the king and the rat ministers in the hall: "Gods and monsters, the republican era, the new heaven and earth in the Central Ocean, the mountains and rivers are bright and beautiful water long, a hundred things are abundant and the four seasons are suitable. The beautiful and harmonious life of the people, the friendship of the neighbors, the transmission of children and grandchildren, and the hope that there will be no beacon. Today, we are asking the officer under the command of the Fire Ant to escort 20 newly invented carts and precious treasures to present them to His Majesty the Rat-headed Ao Dai, with the intention of sharing happiness and fighting together. Other political, economic, and trade matters, as well as warfare and armaments, will be communicated by the special envoy. I am honored! The fire ant marshal Gladin and the military and political state teacher Zhigao Xuanwu summer year The rat warlord Ao Xiong listened, stretched out his mouth, twirling his whiskers: the red-headed monster has always been an enemy of my rat king, repeatedly advised but not listened to, repeatedly recruited but not surrendered, there is a rebellious heart, no intention of submission. But now he offers to give you a gift of treasures, what is the meaning? The rat king issued a letter of war, summoning the two cockroaches of the Central Ocean to present a surrender form and beg to lie down, so as to avoid the arrival of a large army and the destruction of life. This is a wise move to send gifts to our neighbors, and to submit to the north, which is the general trend. The first time I saw this, I was able to get to the top of the list, and I was able to get to the bottom of the list. Now three strong, into the sky there are three days of potential, the ant marshal would like to raise the Hou Yi arrow, three to two. Ao Dai, the king listened, eyes on the twenty large carriage gift, happy to say: show their feelings, build mutual trust, deterred by the army across the river? Show friends Good, respect the throne, fear of millions of majestic army armor? What can we do to communicate with the political, economic, trade and war armaments? In other people's territory, and in the face of the rat's head stern words, aggressive, guess B not panic calmly said: the king's words are not good! Three thousand years of time is like a big river flowing, and the three powers are not a day. I am not afraid of war, but I am tired of war. The fire ant marshal has said that we should make a friendly relationship, and make equal happiness. Therefore, the best policy is to stop the war and shake hands to make peace. The cave was suddenly filled with treasures and 20 new carts, which were unseen by the rat-head. And by the scene demonstration, happy group of rats squealing, dancing. At that time, the rat master treated with courtesy, and arranged to guess B live on the guest house. The soldiers accompanying them all rested. The next day, Ao Xiong Guo Shi said to the Ao Dai king: it seems to make majestic, indeed, is not a fear of war, but the strength of a single soldier in the end, is still unknown, may send soldiers and the battle on the spot. Ao Dai Rat King said: Pingba Colosseum is not operating well, tickets can not be sold, the income dropped sharply. Tomorrow, send people to put up posters, so that the fire head army and my mouse head army fight alone, to see how the strength of both sides? Ao Xiong said: This is very good, I immediately informed the manager of the Colosseum, so that he immediately do so. The Colosseum is located at the side of the Mouse Head Army's martial arts arena in Yunhai Mountain. Gui B received notice that the Rat Head Army was going to have a friendly boxing match with them, and asked the Fire Head Army to prepare. Gui B thought: the wise use their brains, the foolish use their strength, I fire ants is about joint warfare and overall combat power. The rat-headed soldiers are not easy to deal with in this single-armed match. If I lose, I will lose my prestige. If I win, my strength will be revealed. After thinking about it, I came up with a plan. I summoned the team of bodyguard soldiers who were accompanying me and said, "You are all good men and women of Fire Ant, who have been through battle and special training for a long time. I know that you are good at cooperating and working together. Now the rat-headed army wants to fight against us alone, what do you think we should do?

The soldiers said, "Who are we afraid of? Let's fight. Some of them said, "Don't look at them as big and stupid, we are more flexible than them. Guess B said: No losing and no winning, only peace. Each game must be fought for 12 rounds, think about how to deal with it? The soldiers began to scratch their heads, fighting and killing to fight for their lives are not afraid, fighting and, this is too difficult. A fire ant said: small fight big, it is not a quantum, and then to fight and, please teach us how to fight the little military master? Guess B said: the rat-headed monster under the stomach, legs get in that thing called what? "It is the seed transmission sac, right! How to take a beating, in that place to bite a bite, no matter how strong it is not to lose the body will be dizzy. You first let them attack, save strength, to the rat monster panting, in that place to give it a ----" "This can lose or win? " "On points and knockouts, it should be and." "Isn't that against the rules?" "No violation, it's not like there are any rules set up here, just the end, no matter what the means." This guess B has really got the true tradition of Zhigao Guoji. The Colosseum was so crowded that the tickets were sold out two days ago. The black market price was speculated to be doubled. The kings and senior leaders of the rat-headed army came and sat high up on the viewing platform. The surrounding audience was filled with Rathead soldiers and their families, and many of their subjects and submissives wanted to see what the famous fire ant monster could do. To entertain the public, the Colosseum manager arranged a concert followed by a dueling show for love. The rat-headed army versus the ant-headed monster was placed at the end as the grand finale. Singing stars these days because the rat-head manager is too petty and give too little pay, from time to time strike singing. Without the stars, tickets could not be sold, and the concert performance lacked popularity. Today the situation is very different. But the stars still didn't come. The opening act was also in response to the scenery and the manager was also confused. A team of oil crickets came on the stage, and the rat-headed monsters were talking about it, that look, that dress was too uncomfortable. The oil crickets submitted to the rat-headed monsters, and since they have been submissive, they have been sought out from time to time to entertain the public, but they are not very popular. The song started amidst the chaotic complaints. Especially those who paid big bucks for tickets. Jilin! Jilin! Jilin Jilin Jilin! You are beautiful too! I am also beautiful! Singing with your thighs! You twist! I twist my waist! Like the buttocks to please people! This song and dance performance is a broken voice plus kicked legs twisted waist shaking ass, really ugly dead. The next show is too bloody. Duel for love! Too noble, too great and too bloody. Because it is a real fight, are armed with weapons, after the death of a fight, the victor was free to take a wife. This is a show that the Mouse King loves to watch, specially arranged by the winning military. Today's love duel was fought among several captive mantises. The mantis fighters entered the arena very serious, a row will be their wives of female sad and tearful standing in the back of the fighting arena, in the gladiator walked by, was forced to call out a delicate "husband". The husband would shrug his shoulders and act like "Don't worry! I am your husband" kind of attitude. The Ao Dai rat lord and the

Ao Xiong Guo Shi were happy to point out to these gladiators and the females who were forced to be ** or wife. Of course, the fire ant Guai B also sat in the courtesy seat, bright eyes have been scanning the arena, from time to time to delay his soldiers. "Yah!" A cracking killing sound came over. Only to see the two green-backed mantis kill began: the big knife to the head of the wife snatcher cut, for love and sparring prisoners. I have many dolls in my belly, even if I rob a widow that no one wants. Big knife to the front of the love rival cut, in order to pass the seed I must make a death struggle. Everyone because of being a captive slave, not kneeling rather than standing to fight and die. The fight was very intense, more bloody than Spartacus in the Roman Colosseum slave sparring with each other. Broken arms, a small thing. Broken thighs, but also deserved. Blind eyes, it does not matter, the head and neck is broken, desperate to grab a cushion. The wife is watching from the side, the lover may be in tears, for the sweetness of happiness, the dueling arena for love without regret. The fire ants waiting for the match with the rat head at the bottom of the field whispered that the love duel was a wife snatching contest. When they arrived at Rat Head's place, it was really an eye-opening experience. Faced with the upcoming competition, the fire ants were stimulated and started to be brave. The love duel went on one by one until the row of females was finished and no one was left. Just after this bloody duel, the next bloody sergeant's contest began again. Under the escort of a team of fire ants, a fire ant came onto the field with its head held high and its heart set on death. The bloody duel, the smell of death, affected the contestants. Gui B and the contestant finally bit their ears and told them to calm down and not to forget the instructions. The rat-headed sergeant walked out with his head held high to the cheers of the crowd. The fire ants held up their vicious evil heads with high pectoral muscles, and their long, supple legs and feet almost bounced as they stepped into the ring. The rat-headed monster racer looks like a lazy Baji son, some fat and fat. But the body looks quite solid. After he entered the arena, he stretched out his left and right forelimbs, let the audience appreciate the biceps triceps and back muscles, twisted his body and turned his back, and puckered his buttocks a few times, to invite the female audience to reward, indicating a strong fertility. Then he blew his whiskers and glared, raising his arrogant head as if no one else was there. The referee's table sat in a row of several ball-tailed squirrels, trying their best to appear impartial. It was very moralistic. After a squeak from one of the ball-tailed squirrels on the scene, the racers stepped out with a martial step. First came a dismount. The rat head comes in with a hungry tiger pounce, attempting to kill the opponent in one move. The fire ant made a tiger's mouth move and flipped on its heels to avoid it. The rat head made several moves in a row, including **Sounding Ear, Turning Back, Lazy Donkey Roll, and White Ape Moon. The ant-head responded with a long rainbow through the sun, carp jumping Dragon Gate, blind man touching the elephant, and sound striking the west. One is the amazing brute force, strong wind whistling. One is jumping and moving, the needle in the sheep. Two under the field in the circle, the stands but no applause, because there is nothing to kill, so that the spectators feel a little itchy feeling. Not like the love duel as a move to see blood. The rat-headed monster audience could not help themselves and began to squeal with hilarity. "Out with the left jab, carry him for a fall." "Right leg, what's the right leg doing, flying up a foot." "Dull head, not open mouth bite." The shout after shout makes the rat head become prima donna, fire ants were wrestled and wrestled. Ao Dai, the head of the rats, turned his head to Ao Xiong, the master of the kingdom, and said: "The fire ants are not a match for the rats, so they can't compete with my army! Ao Xiong twirled his beard and said: I have a million soldiers who can take down the ant cockroaches like a bag of tricks, and such inferior things can only pay tribute to my kingdom every year. The king is the only one who can take care of them. When the king and the master were pleased with themselves, and the rats in the field were enthusiastic and wanted to cheer the victory, a long scream was heard on the field, and the field was suddenly silenced, and the rats were seen rolling around panting. The gray and white fat belly was first stomped by the fire ant, and then it jumped up and bit, a rotten intestine-like ** son was pulled out. The female rat-heads on the field could not bear to see. The fighting rats howled and tried to throw their opponents off, and the fire ants simply bit and swung. It was like a shrew fighting her husband, using the most effective trick. In the end, the Fire Ants, who had been kicked and swollen by the Fighting Rats, finally gained some face for the ants and the match ended in a draw. The public opinion was that the fire ants were bad. Guess B** with teeth and jaws did not think so: whether it is a bad thing, it depends on what people. The rat and cockroach generation, the usual use of dirty tricks, when the way of others to treat their own body yeah! While the organizers were happy to have organized a tournament with high returns, the audience in the arena suddenly stirred up and smoke and fire rose from the grass pile in one corner of the arena, causing many rats to flee for their lives. Prince Ao Dai's noble rat guards kicked away the rats blocking the exit of the arena, shouting: "Stupid, the king has not yet left, it is your turn to be the first! The king of the country, Ao Xiong, whose face did not change color, said calmly: "Your Majesty, don't panic, it must be the special soldiers of the cockroach head who are mixed in again. "Couldn't it be the fire-headed monster?" "The ant monster is sending an ambassador to send a gift, not enough to break the attack on us, it seems that we have to raise an army to destroy that cockroach head bad seed first." At this moment, a Jinmao rat imperial guard came to report that the Colosseum guards killed several cockroach-headed oil-feathered special soldiers and captured one. Prince Ao Dai called a military meeting with Ao Xiong Guo Shi the day after he was shocked, focusing on the conquest of the cockroach head in Sancha Kou. The fire ant envoy was also invited to attend the meeting because he had sent a heavy gift. The Chinese government said, "The cockroaches at Sanchakou have not responded to the war letter sent by the rat lord of Yunhai Mountain Range, and they are obviously contemptuous. Now, your ambassador from Erjiang is visiting us, and he is willing to kill the cockroach head of Sancha River with Yunhai Mountain Ridge. I would like to hear more about it. Gui B said: "By the order of the Marshal's Office, it is the best policy to have good neighborliness and friendship as the warfare does not stop and the lives are ruined. The rat king's hospitality, the master of the country to help, the small ambassador has reached the upper orders, the next day will return to the two rivers. The Mouse King will attack the cockroach-headed army, and our ant-headed army will respond to it. The second river Linglong Pass is my border defense important place, willing to share the risk of the pass with the rat **, the army is over, support food and pay, send troops to escort. Ao Dai, the king heard the great joy said: If you can do so, very much to my heart. Ao Xiong said: hesitant, stumbling, is the majestic division is not, when the opportunity to make a decision, righteousness, is the cause of victory. Linglong Pass important place, my rat army lend way to travel, hope that the two river ant marshal abide by the agreement. Guess B: I wonder when the rat army will enter the Sancha River? Ao Xiong: The moon and stars are scarce, the sound of chickens and dogs. The army will go out of the mountains and run across the border. Guess B: The moon is full and the light shines on the Ping River. The cockroaches were eliminated by the Sancha River. The two of them immediately high-fived each other, agreed on a code word, and went as scheduled.

Chapter 10

Gui B returned to the camp after his errand to reply to the mission to Zhigao Guoji and briefly recounted what had happened. Zhigao reported the situation to Marshal Gradin and said to the Marshal: The moon and the stars were thin, and the rat army was crossing the border. It was the right strategy to lure the enemy at Sancha River. At that time, the rat army will take over the Linglong Pass in the name of transit. The rat army will be infected with the plague as soon as they are deployed, and the plague will spread to the whole army as they march back and forth. The plague and the flooding of the rat army will be superimposed on each other, and the death of the rat army will not be far away! Marshal Gladin said: "The rat army claims to be millions of soldiers and generals, my two rivers army to complete its success in one battle, need the perfect timing, location and people and perfect cooperation. It must be carefully planned and calculated. The king's head is a swine's head, a rat's eye, and an ill-conceived mind, and Ao Xiong is a man of great ambition and little intelligence. At the order of the day, the waterfall of the dumb lake rolled up a thousand piles of snow, washed away the sludge and water, and buried the rat and cockroach army in the sea. The remaining remnants of the army, the plague of the epidemic to kill, and then there is a leak of fish, special break attack soldiers to destroy. After finishing his speech, Zhigao looked up to the sky and laughed. The tent, a great wind hunting and river turbulence, Jingo Yang and the enemy chills the majestic strategy. The most important thing is to have a laugh about hunger and cockroach flesh, and a generous hand to drink the blood of the rat's head. Marshal Gladin then issued the following instructions to his generals: "Ask the engineering ants, General Blackfire, to secretly open the dumb lake tunnel on the night of the full moon, and make sure the flooding occurs that night." "General Brightfire, the special warfare ant, will bury the plague voodoo in the key pass of Linglong Pass and act on the rat army." "Ask the flying ants, General Minghuang, to descend into the caves of the cloud and sea mountains where the rats' heads are cooped up, and destroy the remaining rats." "The sea battle ants fluorescent fire general, run to bordering the two rivers three branch river vast grass swamp, sweep the rat cockroach head remnants." Then many other military affairs were distributed. All the generals responded to the order and went away. The last general, seeing that all the generals had received orders and gone away, but he was standing in the place without receiving orders, he grimaced and twisted his jaws and said: "Why does the last general not have orders, I hope the marshal will give orders. Zhigao recruited him to the side tent, to it solemnly commanded: General do not need to be anxious, there is a huge military situation by you take charge. You lead a large army to guard the two rivers upstream of the dumb lake east dumb pass. I am sure that the rat's head will be faithless, as long as the attack, kill it on the spot, so that it has no return. The general was ordered to leave. The moon was about to be full at the edge of the golden encrustation, and the mountain wind was rustling the grass yellow. The mountains were colorless, and the cockroaches were seen in the hazy shadows. Ao Dai, the king of the school field, counted the troops, each rat-headed general and colonel with distinctive armor, spear and spear, the main regiment of rat formation set out. Yunling East Mountain, Yunling West Mountain two rat army, West Mountain troops to the two rivers area Linglong Pass and go, another East Mountain troops east to south directly to the Sancha River gateway to the big oil ponds. The cunning Ao Xiong Guo Shi also assembled a South Mountain Corps to travel westward. The Rat Head not only wanted to take the Fire Ants' stronghold of Linglong Pass, but also wanted to seize the Erjiang hills in one fell swoop to make the Fire Ants lose their base and become homeless roaming bandits. The goal of the Rat Head Nanshan Corps was the Mute Pass on the shore of Mute Lake. Since the Cockroach Head Army Governor You You and the White Ruler Great Wisdom had been spending their time since they got a battalion of beautiful girls from the State Master of Ji Gao, they finally thought of joining forces with the Ant Head Army to fight against the Rat Head Army. The special warfare soldier commander had many news to report, one of which was that the Rat Head was going to launch a big army to conquer the Sancha River area in the near future, to slaughter the cockroach head army. You You You Dude shouted: just about to go to exterminate, they sent themselves to the door looking for death! The old white moth demon said: "The rat head is used to bluffing tricks, before the war letter, killing, now want to send troops to challenge, our army should be with the headache, in order to respond to the wisdom of the high ants head of the alliance. The Sancha River area is a fertile plain with rich crops and rich products. The cockroach-head army was stationed on the dam. Fortifications were built between the ditches. Jianbiya, the governor's residence of the cockroach commander Youyou, is a large house with fertile land and beautiful water. It is buried deep under the cliffs of the ** wall. The walls are painted with gold, the beams are painted with silver, and the interior is decorated with opulence. The cockroach-headed imperial army is well versed in alley warfare, night warfare, fortress warfare, jungle warfare and other special combat essentials, jungle and fortress tunnels, stacks, ditches, caves overlapping countless. At the command, the enemy is killed in the invisible. The invaders will be killed under the gully and the cliff. The legion is on the march, and a great battle is about to begin. The cockroach head governor's office mobilized all the young and strong to participate in digging tunnels for the base. The underground defense system was improved. In the key passes, such as Green Cliff, Narrow Cliff, Broken Cliff, Bald Cliff, Cliff, Reed Rock, Three Stars Rock, Quyun Cave, Black Wind Cave, etc., seven caves, eight rocks and nine cliffs were interconnected and barricaded to prevent wind, water and fire. Day and night, dusk and dawn, but see the cockroach flow of traffic, lights, grass and mud filled in the road, making the dust flying dark. The cockroach-headed army did make the war preparations sound, and all the people were united in making the same enemy, and the governor of Yuyao, the long white ruler of wisdom, had won the hearts of the people. The moon will be full on the day, the cockroach-headed army in the Youyou deputy governor of the White Ruler think-tank group assisted by the formation of soldiers in the Qingbiya three stars rock black wind cave line. Gathering can defend the gateway to Dayutang, and scattering can be divided into a combined attack on the border of Linglong Pass. Car clattering horse Xiao Xiao, the rat-headed army east and west of the two large army is vast, like the rat's head pointed mouth two tiger teeth straight into the Hecha plain. In order to lure the enemy deeper, they implemented the wall to withdraw from the Linglong Pass and clear the field. The food processing plant was constantly cooking around the clock, preparing food for the army's long-distance raids behind enemy lines. The moon was not yet full and the light was dark when several squads of 1,000 men from the ant-head army, led by their chiefs, left the Linglong Pass and climbed the mountains unnoticed. The engineering soldiers on the shore of the dumb lake are standing by to defend the thousand-year project that has been kept secret for many years, and as soon as the marshal gives the order to open the gates and release the water, the roaring river will rush forward to swish the millions of rat cockroaches gathered downstream for the dueling majors. The moon is getting fuller and fuller, and there is a stem of goose feather difference. At the mouth of the tunnel in the dumb lake, a cockroach-headed task force and rat-headed squad were advancing from different directions to the mountain pass on the second side. The wind in the valley began to breathe blood. The thousand-year-old Mute Lake project had done the best job of keeping secrets, but there were still times when secrets were leaked. On the eve of the rat-cockroach showdown and the big sneak attack, the long-rumored dumb lake project became a psychological barrier to the rat- and cockroach-head showdown. As a precaution, both sides sent special forces to prepare for a surprise attack on the locations around the dumb lake in order to eliminate all possible unfavorable factors. It was also the heavy responsibility of the Fire Ant Engineering Guard Regiment to hang the incoming special forces. The major passes, mountain passes, valleys, reeds, avenues, trails, secret paths, and mountain ranges around Mute Lake are guarded by year-round ant heads. For a thousand years, the system has been uninterrupted. Such a Tunghu system was imitated by later generations as a Tuntian system, or a construction corps or something. The key is the tunnel entrance, the highway prepared by the fire ants for the water dragon king. Someday good power to strike the plain downstream. Cockroach head rat head are superior to close combat night battle broken attack war. They are also masters in single combat. Ant head is good at playing synthetic warfare, out of patrol are small units. The mountain pass has the sound of a sissy, like the wind blowing falling leaves, and like thatch fall and sway from side to side. There is the slightest change in temperature, like the difference between the first moon and the full moon, and like the difference between the shade under the dead leaves and the warmth of the cave walls. Only the fire ants can perceive it. "That! Muzzle!" The fire ant soldier who was on sentry duty gave a roar. The sharp voice cut through the quiet of the night under the starlight. The current ones were a couple of rat-headed special forces soldiers who had been suddenly startled. One of the inexperienced mice "squeaked" and leaked the bottom. At the same time, a stream of urine came out. "Ducks..." There was a loud sound of vibrating feathers. A group of fire-feathered ant-heads flew at the mice trying to approach and attack the fortress. The night was cool as water and the fight was hotly contested. In addition to the sound of ping-ponging weapons**, there was also the sound of squeaking and chattering tussles. A fire ant quickly arrived at the near camp to recruit a group of ant-headed soldiers, and instantly the rat-headed were injured! Rip live!" The group of soldiers, jumping and skipping towards the dark shadow. The first of these is a few of the most popular and popular of all the other soldiers. The rat-headed orthopedic special forces panting each pulled away from the other, some finally collapsed. The ant-headed soldiers flew after them closer. The rat-headed soldier got sad and squeaked, asking for support from his accomplices: "For the sake of the brothers of the robe, pull a brother!" The selfish rat-headed accomplice listened and turned around and said: "Man, if you don't succeed, you'll become a man! While the ants and rats were fighting to the death, several cockroach-headed soldiers entered the mute lake tunnel, which was under strict control of the ants' heads, with extraordinary skill. They saw a large number of ants pulling up the gate. "Ah ah not good, big water is coming, the Dragon King is departing." As if there was a dull thunder, all the cockroach heads, including the ones pulling up the gate, were swept away by the flood. The dumb lake was released. This is an extraordinary and memorable day. On this day, the moon was full and the rats and cockroaches dueled in the lower alluvial plain of the Second River Basin. It was the harvest season when the grain was ripe and the fish were fat. The fruit pulp was full of branches and the melons were fragrant and fell. In the manors of the landed gentry, in the mansions of the princes and noble relatives, there was singing and dancing and exchanging of glasses to celebrate the northward movement of the king's division. The men, the warriors, joined the Northern Expeditionary Army. All the barracks in the seven caves, eight rocks and nine cliffs, except the garrison troops, were transferred into the dueling armies. The men and horses from both sides, on one side, cast whips to the Se River, and on the other side, cast whips to the Se River. Both are hundreds of thousands, into millions of people. Also add their own subservient slave troops, foreign mercenary troops, friendly allied troops. The rat-headed army really as Zhi Gao said, when borrowing the way Linglong Pass in one fell swoop to seize the pass, and then east into the Sancha River. The eastern army made a pincer-shaped detour against the advance. Both sides fought and killed to the darkness of the sky and the full moon. The Purple Fire General, the head of the ants, set up his troops at Mute Pass and strangled the rat-headed army that tried to attack the rear of the fire ants. The four square formations of the flying feathered ant-head expeditionary army of nearly ten thousand people descended straight to the Cloud Sea Mountain Ridge and surrounded the Cloud Sea Cave, wanting to make the battle of decapitation, so anxious that Prince Ao Dai wanted to hang his neck in the back garden. After the dumb lake flooding, several sections of driftwood boats and behind the bamboo raft reed boats, filled with ants head of the eastward force, joined the General Assembly battle. Mute Lake tunnel released flood waters flooded the downstream alluvial plain. The rat-headed and cockroach-headed armies, each numbering nearly a million, were all swept into the sea. The cockroach-headed gentry in the fertile plain and the original seven caves, eight rocks and nine cliff defenses were permanently sealed into the ground due to the deposition of silt. A few of the rat and cockroach soldiers and generals who were floating and sinking were struggling to survive in the **Zeeland. When they saw the ant-headed monsters coming on the waves in canoes, reed-leaf boats and bamboo canoes, they thought that their savior had arrived, and they all reached out and leaned on them. The next thing they knew was that there would be a ruthless killing. The fire ants were all over the place, and the rat-headed cockroaches were in the flood, screaming at the sky and the earth. There was nothing left to do but to die. "Raise your hands in surrender and shout long live the Fire Ant Era to the ship." "Those who shout long live the Fire Ant Era come aboard." All that could be heard was a chorus of shouts: Long live the Fire Ant Era. The rat heads and cockroach heads all surrendered in front of the brightly shining war swords. There were also a few soldiers who had experienced the oceanic battle of rat-heads and cockroaches, and those who were ashamed to shout "Long live the ant-heads" were either killed by the swords of the ant-heads or swept into the sea by the rapids, and merged into the endless white waves. Afterwards, countless azaleas bloomed on the plain, as if in memory of the innocent soldiers who died in the battle. The rat-headed coiled land of the Cloud Sea Mountain Range, along with the advance party of the flying feathered ant-headed expeditionary army. Zhigao Guoji sent follow-up troops to reinforce. Seven and eight rat-headed army in a neat and orderly scale corps strike, have hidden into the mountains to play guerrilla, into a strand of scattered bandits.

Chapter 11

The expeditionary corps led by Prince Constantine arrived at the Mid-Ocean Continent. That was the horizon, and further past that, there should be the first to the enemy conquest of fire ants troops to guide the ocean surface to meet. The wind blew the legion towards a port castle that had been occupied by a rat-headed monster. The legion of ant-heads who had been waiting for three days and nights in the offshore ocean were impatient. King Constantine ordered the bronze head elder, who was in charge of the special forces, to lead a small group to try to land. The stars and the moon had light and the long night had no dreams. The Copperhead Elder went with orders. A group of eighteen warriors sat in a lighted straw boat lowered by the ship. They arrived at the shore without a sound. The rat's eyes were not bright. Although the rat head has become a monster, still has an innate insurmountable genetic. The lookout post was facing the ocean in the night, and it was too foggy to see what was going on. The chief of the post short tail Ken a piece of meat bone, while grinding the long pointed rat teeth said: the sky is pale, the night is vast, there is my rat head good son, the sea border bandits dare not come, the post happy like heaven. The reason for the current happiness must be a piece of meat and bones to chew. Another rat head said: do not rely on father, do not rely on mother, like to be a soldier to fight guns. Have to eat, have fun, every day to wait for the payroll. The rat monster's food and pay is often a dead bird. Fire ants eighteen warriors to the rat monster post under the cliff, with first-class climbing kung fu quickly up to the top. The fire ants heard the self-muttering of the rat-heads who lay waiting for their rations to be paid, happy as heaven. Copperhead decided to touch this post to open the way for the army. Quietly to the accompanying eighteen warriors said: fuck them. There was a coast guard unit of the Rat Head army in the harbor castle. The captured rat-heads at the post confessed everything in order to save their lives. But they did not yet know that the great battle of Mid-Ocean, which would decide their fate, had already taken place. Prince Constantine commanded the expeditionary force to carry out nothing more than a battle for the port castle. But this castle is a strategic place, customs pass, but also a prosperous economic and military stronghold of the rat's head. The castle keeper is a party vassal rat-headed golden-haired general with 3,000 soldiers under him. With the advantage of geography, the fortress blocked the main road from the sea to the inland. However, as long as they paid for the road, many pirates could still pass through this road to do business. For the expeditionary force, the only way was to remove the castle. The prisoner of the post, the rat-headed Shorty, was brought to the tent of the expeditionary force, where he was interrogated by the silver-headed elders of the ant army and told to lead the way and go to the castle to persuade General Golden Mao to submit. As a sign of generosity to the captive, the silver-headed elder had a plate of seafood brought by the ship thrown to him. The rat-head ate it with great relish, forgetting the shame of being a prisoner, and sang a "happy song". The sky is pale, the night is vast, there is my rat head good boy. The sea bandits are coming, surrender with your hands up is the easiest thing to do. The moon is bright, the sea breeze is cool, eat, drink and sleep well. I paid for the passage first, so that we could not be busy. The next day, with the moon shining brightly and the gulls flying south, the rat-headed short hair set out with the ant-headed vanguard battalion. The castle observation school rushed to tell General Golden Hair. General Golden Hair took his men up to the castle to watch. But see not far below the city on the road, dust, a vast army of fire-colored winding, to the approach, only to see the marching banner written on a bucket of fire words. Golden hair shook a ** Phi battle robe said: by the sea border and come, is certainly a new landing of the expeditionary army of ants head. Quickly send someone to the cloud sea cave Ao Dai The king reported, requesting reinforcements. A staff officer listened and quickly sent someone. "Carry the general master's weapons up." Two sergeants came carrying a zhangbaoshan axe. Jin Mao took the axe, paused at the top of the city, and shouted boldly to the outside of the city, "Tally! Listen to the ant-heads below the city, go back to your home, or the rat-head army will kill you without return. A gray rat came out of the ants' formation with a cowering head and shouted up to the city: "General! The chief of the coast post, Short Hair, has been forced to surrender, and they insisted that I deliver the message. If you surrender and offer the city, you are guaranteed a life of pleasure. Golden Hair heard the angry scolding: good shameless thing, still dare to come to the city under the Lusu, caught you will be broken into pieces. Short hair full of energy said: General do not know, when the official is only to get rich, my filial piety to the general merchants passing through the road money is not less? If you do not open the gates, I will immediately go to the king to report you. Golden Hair heard, all angry, the whole body of the mouse hair discolored, said: you bastard. Embezzlement and betrayal of the country are two different crimes, you dare to mix them up. I have to defend my country to the death even if I am corrupt. The silver-headed elder next to Short Hair shouted, "Admire the courageous loyalty of General Rat! Today to advise the eight words of truth. Golden hair: this general master does not want to listen to you and other nonsense. Elders said: merit award, a badge. Do not offer the city, lose your head. Golden Hair said: This general has the responsibility to defend the city, will drive the ant head down to the sea. A junior colonel hurriedly came to report to Jin Mao said: bad, our army defeated Sancha River mouth, and cockroach head million ** die. Golden Mao listened to the bluff as pale as dirt said: nonsense. Little school: ants head army open dumb lake flood waters, three branch river meeting rat cockroach two armies all drowned in the plain river network area. Elders shouted at the bottom of the city: the city's generals listen, the eight words of truth is only those who know the time are handsome. If you do not understand, the city will be broken and suffer. Short hair said: the general dedicated the city, but also as a general, the small also as a post chief. Buy money as usual filial piety a lot. Short hair is talking, the castle "whoosh" shot down an arrow, hitting short hair throat, short hair seriously wounded fell to the ground, cramps will die when far pointing to the golden hair spurting blood said: greedy to take the murderer to silence! General Golden Hair said: In addition to the pickled villain, the General can open the door to accept surrender. Rat head of a million troops drowned in the flood waters, General Golden Hair listened to no longer interested in war. The instinct of the rat's head is greed for life and death, selfishness and self-interest. After killing the short hair who had laughed at him, and covering up the name of corruption, he had nothing more in mind. He decided to open the door and offer the city. The silver-headed elders were overjoyed. The army then entered the city. Three thousand rat-headed soldiers all surrendered. A few days later, Prince Constantine and Marshal Gradin met at the foot of the half-slope of the Erjiang hills. The four elders of the State Master Zhigao and the Golden, Silver, Copper and Iron issued a notice of the decisive victory in the Sino-Oceanic War, which read as follows: "The fertile land of the Sino-Oceanic region, with its beautiful mountains and rivers, is now united with the prosperity of living beings. Flying birds and beasts, rats and cockroaches, mud and turtle armor, bow down and submit. The fire ants are the leaders of the great path, and the fire ants are the ones who do the good deeds. The great evil is eliminated by the fire ants, and the loyal subjects are all for you. There are proud sons from generation to generation, and a new era is opening for the ant-headed king. The star lord of creation smiles, and the fire-colored banner flutters high. 80,000 miles of clouds and the moon, the ocean, four continents, wind, snow and frost, tossing clouds and water without anger, the sky alone to show the proud sun of fire? No more suffering of the living creatures, from now on we will share the good times. After all living creatures are called subordinate, the earth star life test 4 billion years, the earth master fire ants powerful wind far phi. The rats and cockroaches were only kept by the fire ants as food crops, like corn and soybeans, to make three meals a day and daily snacks. The rest of the creatures are at the mercy of the fire ants and are left to languish in remote and inhospitable areas. The world is red, with red clouds in the sky, red colonies on the ground, red nests on the hills, and red sails drifting on the sea. Every place where the fire ants perceive their presence is under their control. With the development of science and technology, the fire ants detect celestial bodies and want to control outer space. At 10,000 ants feet, they can see many big trees in the sky, and at 100,000 ants feet, they can see the mountains that connect to the clouds. They migrate at will and live everywhere. The ants take advantage of the storm tornado to go to farther places, including the islands and reefs floating on the ocean surface. Expeditionary peoples populate the swept colonies, freely grabbing resources and consuming everything. The fire ants' people were satiated, extravagant, and reproductive, singing and dancing everywhere, chanting long live the ants, long live the ant king, and long live the ant god. They have finally fallen from grace and are living in a drunken stupor. With their dominance and lack of compassion for their species, their callousness and self-harm, and their unbridled murderousness, the star lords and gods of creation feel that they have done something wrong again. They were perfect when they were created, but when they entered the terrestrial interface, they were insane and insane. The once energetic and aggressive nature of the creatures could not hide their arrogant and aggressive nature and their greed and bloodthirsty nature. The Fire Ants' observatory at the Prosperity Tree allowed them to gradually understand the truth of the universe and to sense their own crisis. A space that cannot be measured by ants' ruler, ants' time, ants' space, and the existence of Hercules, whose intelligence is billions of times higher, these rulers of outer space are the real kings of the world. But they have not had time to fully realize the net, God came with a light blow, instantly the sky fire rolled, death enveloped everything, fire ants were all destroyed. The Fire Ants' unparalleled history of conquest, the glory of the Fire Ant Throne, was forever recorded in the history books, but at the same time, the Fire Ants perished and fell into silence. Most of the fire ants entered the oil and gas phase of the Earth's core, and a few of them became fossilized and fossilized in the crust of the Earth's mantle. In the Palace of No Phase at the top of the Brightness of the Immeasurable Mountain. The valley around the flow of light echoes, birdsong and flowers, ten thousand animals wander. Clouds, trees, and fog are all around the palace. The emperor of Wushang Khao was on a tour here, preparing to call a meeting. The four-faced star ruler, the duty officer, went to the mirror platform to inform the star rulers, the emperor and the gods to attend the meeting. The mirror can see the 360-dimensional bright dark matter world of the four faces and nine phases. The Longevity Examination Heavenly Emperor was sitting on the Starry Platform with his face like the full moon, holding the Spiritual Realm Book in his hand and squinting his eyes. When he opened his eyes, the four-faced star ruler sent a command on the phase mirror of the mirror summoning platform. The heavenly emperor's eyes opened and closed nine times, and then nine phase emperors and venerable gods came to the Palace of the Phaseless. These allies came from far away and all had different means of transportation. But a common characteristic is that they make good use of photons. The ones from the dark matter world are good at using plutons. The collection of photons and meditrons transforms into a thousand different and magnificent forms. The experience of riding these streams of light and stardust allows the rider to enter a state of phantomlessness again and again. These nine Star Sovereign Phase Emperors and Dignified Gods, they are the Star Sovereign of Creation, the Primordial Star Sovereign, the Phase Sovereign with Phase, the Phase Sovereign without Phase, the Phase Sovereign of Qi, the Dignified God of Joy, the Dignified God of Punishment and Fear, the Dignified God of Creation, and the Dignified God of Harmony. Seeing the arrival of the gods, the full-moon emperor showed his kindness and joy and bowed deeply to all of them. The gods also and the heavenly emperor and worship, mouth: I alliance emperor longevity, heavenly life without examination! Heavenly Emperor in the temple chair sleeve robe a wave: the Lord as the guests, each gentleman at will.

Chapter 12

The gods were sitting or lying down, standing or leaning around the emperor, each gazing at the emperor's gaze, the beginning of a tour of outer space that had nothing to do with the fire ant century. The Emperor gently slides his finger through the Spiritual Realm Book. In his mind's eye, the Emperor displayed the past and future stardust scenes of infinite time and space, instantly outlining and analyzing them in detail. The Heavenly Emperor pinched and folded a few fingers a few times and stopped at the Auxiliary Galaxy Solar Constellation. The emperor of the phase immediately came out of the class and said: the solar constellation is still in its prime, the phase potential is far ahead, the Milky Way has a dragon flying over, only the solar constellation has the intention to follow, if left alone, or into the no phase. Its gang brothers will also be similar. No phase emperor rose and said: where there are constellations want to enter the phase, all because of their emotional depression, there is a phase star potential lack of gravity, the emperor if you give the sun ruler a beautiful girl, so that his heart is attached, will not go! The Emperor moved his finger again. Creation star ruler said: one like twins, the sun star ruler is a multi-twins, good beauty girl people. The original star ruler said: back in the year of the creation of the star, the sun ruler is actually from the finger leak, the Milky Way is my belt, the sun ruler still has the texture of the belt, I should pick it up. Under the jurisdiction of the emperor, the god of joy rose and bowed to the emperor and the emperor, saying: "The two emperors are on top, I am under the sun star ruler, so I can prove that the sun ruler has no intention of leaving the virtue. His heart is like the water of the ancient well, no waves. The Milky Way dragon is still in the unknown phase of the qi, I hope the two emperors to understand. The creation of the gods: under the command of the sun star, worship the benevolence of the sun star, the god of creation has become, so far more than a hundred million years, has reached a great deal of ocean! In the past billions of years, the creation of countless things, repeatedly tried and failed. In the spirit of failure is the mother of success, now finally success, it is not easy to get, I hope beg not to waste. The Heavenly Emperor held the Spiritual Realm Book in his hand and moved his fingers a few more times. The God of Harmony said: I specialize in the Earth Star, the God of creation, the nature of a thousand changes, there are a lot of cattle and hair, I spent nine cattle and two tigers to make the harmonious coexistence, it is not easy, when the treasure. The emperor said: no life test reincarnation, the earth star creation dazzling, I do not know how many, hope that the creation of the gods to elaborate and hear. The God of creation stretched out one hand, look at the five nails, to a nail, with the tongue ** **, and then look at the mirror image: "the emperor gods, the small gods absorb the essence of the sun and the moon, the spirit of heaven and earth, the wide range of interstellar dust, rain and dew, the creation of things without life test. The earliest has been the fire pulp, the core, the second is the gas wrapped in the belly, the next in the form of oil and charcoal, cloaked in again and again under the rock layer, and again, fallen to the surface, mountains, rivers, territory, sea border, vast and infinite." "How many fire ants have been disturbing the earth for a long time?" "The broad and shallow period, belonging to the oil and charcoal era." The emperor moved his finger again, pointing to the spirit realm book: hidden fine music, between the smell of flowers, is very beautiful, the night is what year? "Now belongs to the earth's surface spirit long-term human form era, to billions of years round era, only within a round. The age of wisdom years. According to the year of humanoid intelligence, more than a thousand years have passed since then." "What is the relationship between the fire ants and the wisdom year?" "The small gods created the fire ants, and their dominant form is more than the same as that of the intelligent man. It has a thin waist and large hips, six feet long and three wide hips. There are second-hand six feet, the ground and tail hip into a triangular pile shape, stable as Tarzan. Walking swiftly, strong, the back can produce wings, wings fly a thousand feet over the hillock without gasping, the heart is not false. The head is large and smart, eyes like a torch, far-sighted, to be teleported and the same kind of information exchange, double jaws such as sharp edges can cut any large creatures and hard * * * body. The saliva is so poisonous that the touch of it makes the rest of the creatures unconscious, and is treated as a meal on the plate. Females have countless eggs in their rump, and in addition to eating and drinking, they are happy to mate with each other and produce hundreds of babies daily. Therefore, reproduction is rapid, intelligent, brave and good at fighting, the world is unmatched, to dominate a period. In the past, in the wisdom of the year, the surviving fire ant heirs have been reptiles, only hibernating in the mountains and cracks, not the past, only with other creatures remaining saliva to survive, but the population is still huge, desperate to rise again. "The music, music, singing and dancing are all peaceful and quiet. Why is there a clanging sound of gold." "The small gods of creation have flaws, so that the primates fight endlessly, such as the permanent past, will follow the punishment, step fire ants overthrow." The four gods of creation, joy, punishment, and harmony said: "The gods have failed in their duty, so that people are good at playing, greedy for treasures, lost in harmony, joy is not as good as the masses, is also a fault, I hope the emperor of heaven severe punishment. The emperor laughed and said, "Why not? I hope the emperor will punish me severely. This is the essence of reincarnation. At this time, the four-faced astrologer came from the mirror platform and said: "There is a wise man from the earth star who is in the harem of the king of the Chen Kingdom in the Central Plains, showing the 24 concubines in Taiji Paradise, with music and singing and dancing. I would like to ask the emperor to look at it. The Creator God was about to say a few more words on the subject when a star lord of the Earth suddenly spoke to the Emperor: "Homo sapiens intelligence exploration has been out of the jurisdiction of the Sun King, and because of the control of space technology, there are signs of mutual destruction. They want to destroy my home? They are really following the footsteps of the billions of creatures, the fire ants. The emperor of heaven asked the creator: there is such a phenomenon? The Creator said: "The Earth Star Lord is under the jurisdiction of the gods and the managers of the gods, we should do our best to coordinate, so that the Earth Star Lord will not worry. The star-appointed official said: "The mirror image of the air is depressed, the clouds are vaporized, and there are tomb gods and monsters ravaging. The Heavenly Emperor said: Four gods of the Earth Star! The God of Creation, the God of Joy, the God of Harmony, and the God of Punishment and Fear responded in unison: We are here! "The king of the Chen Kingdom Taiji Paradise twenty-four concubines of the sexy story map, although in the intelligent people a thousand years ago, the love of heaven and earth, love and hate, but there is still something to take, can warn the current intelligent people of the Earth Star changes. The fire ants are overly multiplied, and the throne is cold and uncontrollable, so even though they are in the mantle, the gods of creation should hide their affairs so that they do not spread again. The star ruler of the gods, nothing to do, except doze at the head of the mountain, phase into the phase of no phase, gas line ring patrol, strict enforcement of the laws of heaven." "There is a phase into the phase without a phase, the primordial five emperors of creation travel with me to patrol the star domain of the Longevity Test, so that the star rulers of the extreme domain can observe the law and make the Heavenly Court peaceful." All the star gods and rulers said they respected the order. In an instant, the meeting of the heavenly emperors at the top of the Light of the Immeasurable Mountain ended, and the images disappeared without a trace, leaving only the curling auspicious clouds flowing. When the descendants of the fire ants remaining on the Earth planet groveled and struggled to enter the age of intelligent humans, they became tiny reptiles. After baking and freezing for hundreds of millions of years, it has developed an invincible body. One day it felt a slight vibration in the topaz, so it gently struck the topaz with its tentacles, and accidentally heard the Emperor and the star rulers parade around and discuss many past and present events. When he heard this, he was overjoyed and thought he had an opportunity. He had heard that a stone monkey had caused a big disturbance in the Heavenly Palace and disturbed the Heavenly Emperor. It was time for him to go out and make a breakthrough. He thought that since he was a wise man in Taiji Paradise, he had been petrified for a long time and his skills were limited, so he should go to the back garden of King Chen's house in Central China to experience the wisdom of life. The king's body is so beautiful that he will be able to make those wise men's emotions and desires more interesting, so that he can have more babies with the joy of mating. The ant king thought and turned around, but when he didn't move, his muscles and bones rusted and he couldn't move a bit. He thought, "If we want to go out of the mountain, we must spare no blood. So it carried its head and struggled with air, and instantly the debris flew and the armor broke. The ant king rolled out of the rock crevice and rolled to the bottom of the mountain, only to be blocked by a tree branch. The ant king inhaled the fresh air that it had not seen for a long time, and it developed at once, its body expanded like blowing air. It took a look in the lake water near the tree and saw a beautiful reflection. It was six feet long, with four wide hips and two big, watery eyes like lights. When he raised his arms, he saw the flat hair like clouds, and it was one foot long. He picked a fruit from the top of his head and threw it into his mouth. He tried his legs again and felt that his power was endless. He flew up with a sweeping leg and swept a boulder off his feet into the lake with a thump. When the water was stable, I saw that the big buttocks were like a drum, and it became a cushion, with its hind legs bent at the knees and its whole body with its chest and head up. It is a majestic, upright and wise. At this moment, he felt a slight itch on his back and shook his hair a little, and saw that the pair of wings on his back were intact. The ant king gave a boost of energy and flew up to the top of the tree with a buzz. The ant king was so happy that he slowly came down from the tree, but saw many fire ants coming from the roots of the tree and the grass, surrounding him with their beards and jaws, shouting, "Long live our king! The king of the ants stretched out his beard and checked with pheromones, but they were all descendants who had survived hundreds of millions of years ago. "Wow yo yo, how did the descendants become so thin and weak, tiny and not ant-shaped." "The former king, the small ones suffered, we are now the mountain wilderness earth reptiles category, no longer dominate the world epoch touch." The ant king shook his head and wagged his beard, greatly sighed and said: children and grandchildren wait patiently, this great king to turn the tide. The ant king don't fire ant colony, a moment of heart has a kyu hindrance, in the era of intelligent people dominated, I fire ants how to be human rivals? I would like to go to Mount Bu Zhou and learn some skills from the gods and goddesses, so that I can use them on earth to fight against humans. Only then can we manage to rule them. The fire ants have an idea in mind, they are determined to go to find the mountain, the heavenly emperor star ruler gods to rest and doze off in a place of relaxation. The ant king, with his billions of years of cultivation, bent his hips, folded his front legs and sat on his hind legs, erected his forehead antennae and scanned the heavens. When Gong Gong hit Bu Zhou Mountain in anger and the sky collapsed, when Nuwa mended the sky, the fire ants lost the world for a long time, the ant king had also ridiculed the sky collapsed well, hoping that the lofty hillocks would never exist again, so that the sky would lose its support. But the era of the fire ants still disappeared, and the great colony corps was sunk into the core of the star and oiled and vaporized. Now it should not be too difficult to find this uncharted mountain. The fire ant king, who had been a genie for hundreds of years, finally figured out what to do and strengthened his wing feathers. The two are still fighting to the death. The king of the fire ants, who had once dominated the world, was able to kill all the creatures and turn them into a meal on his plate. When they arrived at the bottom of Mount Bu Zhou, they saw black clouds covering the field, the wind roaring and thundering, and Mount Bu Zhou hidden in the clouds, with no top visible. At the bottom of the mountain, two groups of people were fighting in the wilderness. At that time, the two men were fighting in a battle. The two men's hatred for each other has evolved into a battle over who will dominate the New World Era. The angels of light represent the wise men, while the hellish beasts, snakes, insects, and pigeons represent the creatures of hell. The king of the ants, after a tentacle sweep, knew that the hell bully could not defeat the angel of light. But somehow, only a few of the Bright Angels were fighting, while the Hellbenders had so many ants attached to them that even the Fire Ant King was itching to get in on the action. Even the Fire Ant King was anxious to intervene. Therefore, the battle was always a draw, and this battle had been fought for tens of thousands of years. The fire ants watched the battle from the sidelines for many hours. The angel of light is a wise man's method of warfare, concentrating his forces on one point and two sides, encircling warfare, pocket warfare, movement warfare, etc. Unfortunately, there are few people, so he loses from time to time. The first of these is the "Beng Seng" (청청청청청청청청청청), which is a traditional Chinese language instrument.

Chapter 13

The King of Ants had no time to worry and climbed deeper into the mountain, his courage to go up to Buzhou Mountain was irresistible. There were many hidden spirits in the deep mountains and valleys, and the king was exhausted after a short time. A snake spirit blocked the way. As soon as the King's beard waved, he knew that this mountain monster was just a thousand-year-old creature, so he didn't need to pay much attention to it. The snake spirit was voluptuous, beautifully dressed and graceful, and when she saw the Fire Ant's garden buttocks, she was very attractive to him, so she spat out her long tongue as if she was very amorous, wanting to kiss him to meet him. The fire ant was a veteran in love affairs. I was the master of the world back then, but I was reduced to being ** by a thousand year old monster, how could I be embarrassed? The fire ant opened its two jaws and took a bite at the snake spirit's long tongue, immediately taking off a piece of flesh. The snake spirit was so angry that his whole body trembled in pain, and even his tail curled up. He cursed, "Where did you come from, you ungrateful **, treating your kindness like a donkey's liver and lungs. The fire ants said: Listen, when I say something, don't be scared shitless, have you heard of the Fire Ant Era Double Wing King? The snake spirit said, "I know there are ants in the mountains, but they are just trifling people who spend all their time in the crevices of the mountains. The fire ants sneered and said: "The one who is not yet dry, when I dominated the world, your grandfather did not have eggs yet! You know you are molesting the ancestors of your grandmother's grandmother. The snake spirit was immediately scolded and disgraced, so he tried to leave with a red face. "Tally! Stop, give me the way, I want to go to Bu Zhou Mountain you know!" The snake spirit said: Bu Zhou Mountain is a long way away, I only know a rough idea, and never went there. "You just point a direction, wrong back to see I do not take you as a little heart." The fire ants really still have the dominance of the world. The snake spirit couldn't be convinced, even if it was a thousand years old and met with a hundred million years of hard hands, so if it didn't give in to the softness and didn't behave itself, it would have to suffer a loss. The tongue that was bitten has swollen to the point that it can barely fit in the mouth. The sky was getting dark and the mountain wind was full of monopoly. The fire ant was so tired of climbing the mountain that it was shaking and panting, and it stopped under a convex rock with a lot of steps. After a long journey, it sweetly went to sleep. Several black ants were crawling around looking for food and crawled under this rock face. The black ants circled around this living creature, which looked like a similar one, and smelled only a fragrance of meat. One of the big black ants, suspected to be the foreman or something, could not help the fragrance of meat**, and drops of saliva came out of its mouth and said, "Let's get some to taste first. He opened his mouth and took a bite. The sleeping fire ants were sizzled and woke up suddenly. When he opened his eyes, he saw several large black-headed ants circling around him, disturbing his dream. The fire ant was furious and lifted its leg, kicking the black ant to the ground. It is common for ants to be kicked over when they are looking for food, so the black ant was not angry and said to some of its companions, "This worm is full of vitality and tastes delicious. Several ants set up their stance and were ready to take a bite first. The fire ants were completely disturbed and said to the descendants of the ethnic minorities, "Look at the target first, okay? I am your grandfather, don't you know me? This message was confirmed by the descendants, and several black ants nodded and nodded after moving their tentacles, and one of them flew back to report the news. Then they all prostrated on the ground and raised their backs high. The fire ants looked high and wide and put their feet on the back of the black ant king, expressing their satisfaction at their respect and submission. The fire ants were carried back to their nests, where they ate and drank for three days to refresh themselves and then set off again. This time, not only did the fire ant have a guide, but also some bodyguards and a bred turtle worm carried it over a hill before waving goodbye. It was getting colder and colder, and the fire ants could no longer lift their wings, and even if they could take off, they could not fly far. But the fire ant's unyielding will is unshakable. It has an ideal, and the strength of its ideal can endure all hardships and its ambition can withstand unimaginable tests. The rocks on the mountain are slippery and cold, and the wind is so cold that the fire ants often have to hide in the valley to escape the cold when they are tired. Climbing snowy mountains barefoot, have you ever heard of this? But where to find them? In the valley, there was a bear rabbit that had been killed and the meat had been eaten by other animals, but the four bear feet were still intact. The bear paw was delicious, but unfortunately it was a bit smelly, but I didn't care so much. Then I put my foot inside, and although I was a bit angry to wear small shoes, I finally solved the problem of boots. When I looked up at Mount Buzhou, the mountain peaks were still in the clouds. The fire ants stood at the hillock and stomped their feet, "You old monsters, why do you go to those places to rest and doze? A white-headed pale eagle came from the sky and circled around a valley. The eagle flies high, flies far away, and from time to time, it also gives a two whistles, apparently proud and comfortable. Now the king is in trouble, why don't you come and help? "I am the master of the Fire Ant Era, and even if you are the highest flyer, you have submitted to me before, right? Now the king is in trouble, won't you stretch out your claws to help? "The fire ant sent its message from its tentacles to the sky. The eagle is not of the same kind as the fire ant and cannot receive such signals. But the once dominant eagle emits a powerful kingly voice. This sound once made the eagle's ancestors tremble in fear, and passed on such a terrifying genetic code to the next generation. The mountain eagle heard this horrible call. Obediently flapping its wings, the mountain eagle stopped on the rock. "Take me up to the top of Mount Bu Zhou, where the Heavenly Emperor and God rests and dozes." The mountain eagle looked down at this chic and different sized fire ant and nodded. At the top of the Buzhou Mountain, the sky is vast, with streams of light circling around, where the wind, frost, rain and snow do not invade, and the sun is warm as spring. There are several pale boulders, flat as a mat, which are indeed a good place to rest and rest. In this untouched place, the fire ants took advantage of the mountain eagle to reach a rock and crawled around to find a safe and hidden place to wait patiently for the star gods of the upper sky to meet and rest here. "Gods, you will surely come. I am determined to wait until you are all dead. I am the sovereign king of the Fire Ant Era, and I want to restore my glory and power to dominate the world. " The fire ant was mumbling alone. He was blind now, and although he was once a king, he could not see a bit of God's form. In fact, the two gods were sitting on the stone ping not far away playing chess. The God of Creation and the Lord of the Earth Star were playing with each other with wide sleeves and big robes, with cloudy shoes and clean socks, smiling. They heard a voice. Before he could look at them, the God of Creation gave the God of Creation a general. The God of Creation took out a snuff bottle given by the emperor and smiled, saying, "Who is talking there? I was distracted. The god of creation said, "A fire ant made in the distant past is chattering alone. It is not convinced that it has lost! The God of Creation smiled and pointed to the chessboard: The game is not finished yet, so I can't say I lost, can you help it? When the God of Creation saw the Fire Ant's delusional attitude, he said ungraciously, "Your time has been lost, so don't do any more delusional things. "A faint but clear voice sounded in the fire ant's ears. The fire ant looked around and did not see any object. The fire ant was a clever creature and realized that the god was probably close by. He was whispering to him. "If the fire ant can no longer dominate the world, it should at least ** the world, but my ability to dominate the world has not changed. " "A hundred thousand years ago the wise man and a hundred thousand years later the intelligent man, their own creation. Their wisdom is still unpredictable. Your surviving descendants are living strong and co-existing with them, and the dream of a resurrection is illusory. " "In the name of the master of the Fire Ant Era, I ask the gods to give me the opportunity to fight against the Wise Men. Let's see who will win." "Any chance needs to be created by yourself, your toughness and determination to not give in to defeat is the hope to dominate the world. But doing something with little hope will make you suffer. You can spend time with wise people and experience their ability to dominate the world. "In front of the gods, the former world master, the fire ants, could not be proud of themselves. Since you can give the world spring, summer, autumn, winter, wind, rain, thunder and lightning, you might as well give the Fire Ant some new abilities. "Your greatest skill is your fearsome ability to reproduce. You have been fossilized in the topaz rock for hundreds of millions of years, and now that you are back, your skills will not disappear. For the sake of your strong spirit, I have a bag containing all kinds of skills! " "God, where are you, how come I can't see you?" "You do not need to see me, you just need to reach out and touch it." The God of creation said this, "I can't see the bag that contains the master, so how can I touch it?" "You can only touch it once, and you can only take one. If you try to touch it and try to fish in troubled waters and touch more than one, then you will suffer the consequences. Now touch it, there are the skills you want. You've got it! "The fire ant really closed its eyes and stretched out its forearm and grabbed it in the air, thinking that I would touch it one more time and you old monsters could not help me. It caught a verse. When he opened his eyes, he saw the four words "Random Response" written on it. The fire ant held another one in the crevice of its little finger, but when it opened its eyes, it had no words. The fire ant thought, "I'm glad that I can randomly respond to the situation. But what does this piece of white paper without words mean? After thinking about it for a long time, I don't think the white paper means that I was busy and happy for nothing, right? Feeling a bit weak, I tilted my head and swallowed the paper by throwing it into my mouth. The fire ant thought, "If I swallow it, the old monster won't see it and won't know that I have touched one more piece. Now that I can change, let's try it first. What should I change into? Let's change into a bird and fly down the mountain, so as to avoid the hard work of climbing up and down. But then I thought, "It's too bad for me to become a bird to be the king of fire ants, so why don't I turn my wings into the wings of an eagle and fly to the place I want to go? I said "Change!" when I thought of it. The fire ant tried it out on the spot to see if it would work. Sure enough, a pair of feathers on its back became a pair of long and robust wings that could travel thousands of miles. Can it fly? With a single movement of his wings, he flew up into the sky. The fire ant was overjoyed and bowed to a breeze in the sky, saying: "Thank you, Star God, the fire ant. A voice in the air said, "When the battle between the Angel of Light and the Hell Buster was in full swing under the mountain, Gong Gong collapsed a corner of Mount Bu Zhou, and the Goddess of Mercy missed a stone to make up for heaven, which led to a "Stone Story". ". Both books have been etched in the annals of human history. You, who came out of the yellow jade stone, should also behave yourself! "Your God is above, now you have been created, and the fire ants can be randomly changed. I hope you can tell me how to make a "record"." "The king of fire ants has the ability to have sex with big hips, and the ants' cave is full of love stories. There are a lot of flirtatious stories!" When the fire ants heard this, they understood in their hearts that they had the ability to have sex, and they wanted to go to the sex scene of the wise people to compare how to pass on their big hips. This is the way to restore the Fire Ant Era. It is also an opportunity for the story to become a "record" and be recorded in history. The fire ants had a pair of strong wings and came straight down from the top of Bu Zhou Mountain and stopped at the battlefield between the Angel of Light and Hell Hell. Hellblazer shouted: "The bird flying from Mount Bu Zhou will help us win the battle. The angel of light shouted: "The bird cannot help the evil, and vows to defend the light and fight. The fire ants were very angry when they heard that they were the fire ants that had dominated the world, but they said I was a bird. The fire ants were so low-minded that they ignored them. They are fighting for who dominates the world. Light and darkness, righteousness and evil are twins, referencing each other, one cannot be without the other. Who can I help? So I took to my wings and flew away, singing with my mouth: "It comes like a drifting wind, and goes like a cloud of smoke. Thousands of lifetimes, ten thousand years, there are true words of the Lord's destiny. Come like the wind, go like smoke, the world of flowers only leave change.

Printed in the USA
CPSIA information can be obtained
at www.ICGtesting.com
LVHW080821210823
755743LV00006B/419